Zero Hour

Book Two
The Blackout Series

A novel by

Bobby Akart

Copyright Information

© 2016 Bobby Akart Inc. All rights reserved. Except as permitted under the U.S. Copyright Act of 1976, no part of this publication may be reproduced, distributed or transmitted in any form or by any means, or stored in a database or retrieval system, without the prior written permission of Bobby Akart.

Other Works by Amazon Top 50 Author, Bobby Akart

The Doomsday Series

Apocalypse

Haven

Anarchy

Minutemen

Civil War

The Yellowstone Series

Hellfire

Inferno

Fallout

Survival

The Lone Star Series

Axis of Evil

Beyond Borders

Lines in the Sand

Texas Strong

Fifth Column

Suicide Six

The Pandemic Series

Beginnings

The Innocents

Level 6

Quietus

The Blackout Series

36 Hours

Zero Hour

Turning Point

Shiloh Ranch

Hornet's Nest

Devil's Homecoming

The Boston Brahmin Series

The Loyal Nine

Cyber Attack

Martial Law

False Flag

The Mechanics

Choose Freedom

Patriot's Farewell

Seeds of Liberty (Companion Guide)

The Prepping for Tomorrow Series

Cyber Warfare

EMP: Electromagnetic Pulse

Economic Collapse

Dedications

To the love of my life, thank you for making the sacrifices necessary so I may pursue this dream.

To the *Princesses of the Palace*, my little marauders in training, you have no idea how much happiness you bring to your mommy and me.

To my fellow preppers—never be ashamed of adopting a preparedness lifestyle.

ACKNOWLEDGEMENTS

Writing a book that is both informative and entertaining requires a tremendous team effort. Writing is the easy part. For their efforts in making The Blackout Series a reality, I would like to thank Hristo Argirov Kovatliev for his incredible cover art, Pauline Nolet and Sabrina Jean for making my important work reader-friendly, Stef Mcdaid for making this manuscript decipherable on so many formats, and The Team—whose advice, friendship and attention to detail is priceless.

The Blackout Series could not have been written without the tireless counsel and direction from those individuals who shall remain nameless at the Space Weather Prediction Center in Boulder, Colorado and at the Atacama Large Millimeter Array (ALMA) in Chile. Thank you for providing me a portal into your observations and data.

Lastly, a huge thank you to Dr. Tamitha Skov, a friend and social media icon, who is a research scientist at The Aerospace Corporation in Southern California. With her PHD in Geophysics and Space Plasma Physics, she has become a vital resource for amateur astronomers and aurora watchers around the world. Without her insight, The Blackout Series could not have been written. Visit her website at http://www.SpaceWeatherWoman.com.

Thank you!

About the Author

Bobby Akart

Author Bobby Akart has been ranked by Amazon as #55 in its Top 100 list of most popular, bestselling authors. He has achieved recognition as the #1 bestselling Horror Author, #2 bestselling Science Fiction Author, #3 bestselling Religion & Spirituality Author, #6 bestselling Action & Adventure Author, and #7 bestselling Historical Author.

He has written over twenty-six international bestsellers, in nearly fifty fiction and nonfiction genres, including the chart-busting Yellowstone series, the reader-favorite Lone Star series, the critically acclaimed Boston Brahmin series, the bestselling Blackout series, the frighteningly realistic Pandemic series, his highly cited nonfiction Prepping for Tomorrow series, and his latest project—the Doomsday series, seen by many as the horrifying future of our nation if we can't find a way to come together.

His novel *Yellowstone: Fallout* reached the Top 50 on the Amazon bestsellers list and earned him two Kindle All-Star awards for most pages read in a month and most pages read as an author. The Yellowstone series vaulted him to the #1 best selling horror author on Amazon, and the #2 best selling science fiction author.

Bobby has provided his readers a diverse range of topics that are both informative and entertaining. His attention to detail and impeccable research have allowed him to capture the imaginations of his readers through his fictional works and bring them valuable knowledge through his nonfiction books.

SIGN UP for Bobby Akart's mailing list to receive special offers, bonus content, and you'll be the first to receive news about new releases in the Doomsday series:

eepurl.com/bYqq3L

VISIT Amazon.com/BobbyAkart, a dedicated feature page created by Amazon for his work, to view more information on his thriller fiction novels and post-apocalyptic book series, as well as his nonfiction Prepping for Tomorrow series.

Visit Bobby Akart's website for informative blog entries on preparedness, writing, and a behind-the-scenes look into his novels.

BobbyAkart.com

ABOUT THE BLACKOUT SERIES

WHAT WOULD YOU DO
if a voice was screaming in your head - *GET READY . . .*
for a catastrophic event of epic proportions . . .
with no idea where to start . . .
or how, or when?

This is a true story, it just hasn't happened yet.

The characters depicted in The Blackout Series are fictional. The events, however, are based upon fact.

This is not the story of preppers with stockpiles of food, weapons, and a hidden bunker. This is the story of Colton Ryman, his stay-at-home wife, Madison, and their teenage daughter, Alex. In 36 Hours, the Ryman family and the rest of the world will be thrust into the darkness of a post-apocalyptic world.

A catastrophic solar flare, an EMP—a threat from above to America's soft underbelly below—is hurtling toward the Earth.

The Rymans have never heard of preppers and have no concept of what prepping entails. But they're learning, while they run out of time. Their faith will be tested, their freedom will be threatened, but their family will survive.

An EMP, naturally generated from our sun in the form of a solar flare, has happened before, and it will happen again, in only 36 Hours.

This is a story about how our sun, the planet's source of life, can also devastate our modern world. It's a story about panic, chaos, and the final straws that shattered an already thin veneer of civility. It is a warning to us all ...

never underestimate the depravity of man.

What would you do when the clock strikes zero?
Midnight is forever.

Note: This book does not contain strong language. It is intended to entertain and inform audiences of all ages, including teen and young adults. Although some scenes depict the realistic threat our nation faces from a devastating solar flare, and the societal collapse which will result in the aftermath, it does not contain graphic scenes typical of other books in the post-apocalyptic genre.

PREVIOUSLY IN THE BLACKOUT SERIES

The Characters

The Rymans:

Colton – Colton Ryman was in his late thirties. Born and raised in Texas, he was a direct descendant of the Ryman family which built the world renowned Ryman Auditorium music hall in downtown Nashville. His family migrated to Texas from Tennessee with Davy Crockett in the 1800s. The Rymans became prominent in the oil and cattle business and as a result, Colton inherited his skill for negotiating. After college, he landed a position with United Talent, the top agency for the country-western music industry. He eventually became managing partner of the Nashville office. He is married to Madison and they have one child, Alex.

Madison – Madison, in her mid-thirties, is a devout Christian born and raised in Nashville. She grew up a debutante but quickly set her sights on a career in filmmaking. But one fateful day, she was introduced to Colton Ryman and the two fell in love. They had their only child, Alex, which prompted Madison to give up her career in favor of a life raising their daughter and loving her husband—two full time jobs.

Alex – Fifteen-year old Alex, the only child of Colton and Madison Ryman, was a sophomore at Davidson Academy. Despite inheriting her mother's beauty, Alex was not interested in the normal pursuits of teenaged girls which included becoming the prey of teenaged boys. Her interests were golf and science. It was during her favorite class, Astronomy, in which the teacher encouraged his students to become *solar sleuths*, that Alex learned of the potential damage the sun could cause.

Supporting Characters of Importance:

Dr. Andrea Stanford – Director of the Joint Alma Observatory (JAO) Science Team at the Atacama Large Millimeter Array (ALMA) in the high-mountain desert of Peru. She is a graduate of the Harvard-Smithsonian Center for Astrophysics in Cambridge, Massachusetts. Her long-time assistant is Jose Cortez.

Members of the Harding Place Association (HPA) – In 36 Hours, book one of The Blackout Series, Shane Wren and his wife Christie Wren make their first appearance. They have two daughters and live just to the north of the Rymans. Shane Wren is the President of the HPA. In Zero Hour, two other members of the HPA are important players in the saga. Gene Andrews, a former director of compliance with the Internal Revenue Service, and Adam Holder, a former banker, make their appearance. Jimmy Holder, Adam's stepson, is a key player in the story as well.

Primary Scene Locations

Ryman Residence – located on Harding Place in Nashville. It is located approximately two miles east of historic Belle Meade Country Club and just to the west of Lynnwood Boulevard. It is a two-story brick home similar to the one depicted on the cover of Zero Hour.

ALMA - the largest telescope on the planet—the Atacama Large Millimeter Array, or ALMA. It's located at an altitude of over sixteen thousand feet in Atacama, Chile.

Harding Place Neighborhood **–** The portion of the Harding Place Neighborhood depicted in The Blackout Series is bordered by Belle Meade Boulevard to the west, Abbot-Martin Road to the north, Hillsboro Pike to the east, and Tyne Boulevard to the south. Generally, this area is southwest of downtown Nashville in an area known for its historic homes—Belle Meade.

Previously in The Blackout Series

The Blackout Series begins thirty-six hours before a devastating coronal mass ejection strikes the Earth. Dr. Andrea Stanford and her team at ALMA identified the largest solar flare on record—an X-58—hurtling toward the Earth.

This solar flare was many times larger than the Carrington Event of 1859, widely considered the strongest solar event of modern times. Alarm bells were rung by Dr. Stanford and soon eyes at NASA and the Space Weather Prediction Center, SWPC, in Boulder, Colorado, were maintaining a close eye on Active Region 3222—AR3222.

AR3222 was a huge dark coronal hole which has formed on the solar disk. It had grown to encompass the entire northern hemisphere of the sun. As the story begins, AR3222 had only fired off a few minor solar flares, but as the hole in the sun rotated out of view, Dr. Stanford knew it would be back.

That same evening, Colton Ryman was in Dallas, Texas on business. One of his country music clients was being considered for a spot on the upcoming Super Bowl halftime show. Colton participated in a dog-and-pony show hosted by Jerry Jones, owner of the Dallas Cowboys which included tours of the Cowboys' stadium and a concert in downtown Dallas.

Via news reports and text message conversations with Madison, Colton became aware of the unusual solar activity. At first, he brushed off the threat, but as time passed he became more and more convinced.

Madison and Alex were in Nashville going about their normal routine. Alex was the first to ring the alarm that the threat they faced from a major solar storm was real. She tried to raise the level of awareness in her mother, but Madison initially brushed it off as the overactive imagination of a teenage girl.

By noon the next day, all of the Rymans were beginning to see the signs of a potential catastrophic event. While the rest of the country went about its normal routine, Colton, Madison, and Alex made their decision—*Get Ready*!

The initial reports of the solar event were widely downplayed by the media. Even the President refused to raise the alarms for fear of frightening the public unnecessarily. But the Rymans were convinced the threat of a castastrophic solar flare was real, and the three sprung into action.

Colton, unable to catch a flight back to Nashville from Dallas, rented a Corvette and began to race home. Madison, using a valuable resource in the form of a book titled EMP: Electromagnetic Pulse, studied the *preppers checklist* located at the rear of the book which enabled her to apply a common sense approach to getting prepared in a hurry.

Madison pulled Alex out of school and they immediately hit the Kroger grocery store for food and supplies. It was during this shopping expedition that news of the solar flare broke. Society began to collapse rapidly.

After forcing her way out of the grocery store parking lot using her Suburban's bumper to shove a KIA out of the way, Madison and Alex made their way to an ATM. The lines were long, but Madison waited until she could withdraw the cash. However, she let down her guard and was assaulted by a man who tried to steal her money. While the rest of the bank customers stood by and watched, Alex sprung into action with her trusty sand wedge. She beat the man repeatedly until he crawled away—saving her Mom, and the cash.

Meanwhile, Colton's race home—doing over one hundred miles an hour in the rented Corvette—was almost red flagged when he was stopped by an Arkansas State Trooper. While he was waiting for the trooper's deliberation of what to do with Colton, a gunfight ensued between two vehicles in the southbound lane of the interstate. Having bigger fish to fry, the state trooper left Colton alone, who promptly hauled his cookies toward Memphis.

Madison, despite being battered and bruised, elected to make another *run* with Alex. They added to their newly acquired preps but encountered a group of three thugs on the way home. Frightened for their safety, Madison once again used her trusty Suburban bumper to pin one of the attackers against the car in front of her. This brought an abrupt end to the assault.

As Colton drove home, he listened to the scientific experts on the radio broadcasts talking about the potential impact an EMP would have on electronics and vehicles. He learned pre-1970 model cars were more likely to survive the massive pulse of energy associated with an EMP. This knowledge served him well when he stopped at a gas station in eastern Arkansas.

Colton was confronted by three men who took a liking to the shiny red Corvette. Not wanting any trouble, Colton made the deal of a lifetime. He traded the new Vette for a 1969 Jeep Wagoneer. The good ole boys thought they'd gotten the better of the city slicker, but it was they who were hoodooed. Colton took off with his new, old truck and sufficient gas to make it to the house.

Madison's and Alex's exciting day was not over. After dark, a knocking on the door startled them both. It was their friendly neighbors, Shane and Christie Wren. Madison attempted to keep her conversation with them brief, and her newly acquired preps hidden, but the simple mistake of turning on a light revealed her bruised face to the Wrens. The couple immediately suspected Colton of being a wife abuser despite Madison's explanation to the contrary.

After Madison sent the nosy Wrens on their way, she and Alex settled in to watch CNN's coverage of Times Square and the Countdown to Impact Clock. Thousands of people had gathered in New York to witness the apocalypse's arrival. The drama was high as the scene in Times Square was reminiscent of a New Year's Eve countdown without the revelry and deprivation.

The girls anxiously waited as they were unsure of Colton's whereabouts. Then they heard the kitchen door unlock, and Colton entered—reuniting the family. They began to move into the living room when Alex exclaimed, "Hey, look! The clock stopped at zero and nothing happened."

The CNN cameras panned the mass of humanity as a spontaneous eruption of joy and relief filled the packed crowd. The trio of news anchors couldn't contain themselves as they exchanged hugs and handshakes. Jubilation accompanied pandemonium in Times Square, the so-called Center of the Universe, as the bright neon lights from the McDonald's logo to the Bank of America sign continued their dazzling display. Then—

CRACKLE! SIZZLE! SNAP—SNAP—SNAP!

Darkness. Blackout. It was — *Zero Hour.*

The saga continues in ... ZERO HOUR

EPIGRAPH

Here comes the sun. Here comes the sun, and I say, it's all right.
~ the quiet Beatle

*****

Civilization is hideously fragile.
There's not much between us & the horrors underneath, just about a coat of varnish.
~ CP Snow

*****

The time to repair the roof is when the sun is shining.
~ John F. Kennedy

*****

By failing to prepare, you are preparing to fail.
~ Benjamin Franklin

*****

Because you never know when the day before
is the day before.
Prepare for tomorrow!

Zero Hour

Book Two
The Blackout Series

Prologue

Some people had never been in complete darkness—they never had a reason to be. There were always lights—everywhere—spilling from a neighbor's home through your windows or the glow of a nearby town lighting up the horizon. The illumination of cell phones, computer screens, televisions, vehicles, and businesses invaded our surroundings every night—all night.

Most Americans grew up not knowing what complete darkness was. Few had experienced a total blackout, but tonight, at *zero hour*, everyone was. Midnight was forever.

Then there was the silence. Noise could have a harmful effect on your health and psyche. The word *noise* came from a Latin term meaning queasiness or pain. The body reacted immediately and powerfully to the signals transmitted through the ear to the brain. We lived in consistently loud environments, which created chronically elevated levels of stress hormones.

In a world full of commotion, the sudden silence could be frightening. Once, there was the hum of background electronics ranging from kitchen appliances to the fans on computers. In a city environment, the constant sounds emanating from outside—planes, trains, and automobiles—became a way of life. The stillness could be calming, until it made you uncomfortable.

For some, silence wrecked the nerves. It made them uneasy, vulnerable. The quieter it became, the more you could hear. You could hear your breathing or the beating hearts of the loved ones you held tight. The lack of external stimuli quieted your mind and allowed you to focus on what was closest to you.

CHAPTER 1

ZERO HOUR
11:03 p.m., September 8
Ryman Residence
Belle Meade, Tennessee

Alex shrieked at the suddenness of the blackout and the silence. An eerie glimmer of green and blue hues radiated through the transom windows into the Rymans' home, producing a psychedelic glow inside.

Colton hugged his daughter and reassured her. "It's okay, honey. We're all here together."

"My God, Colton," Madison whispered as if hushed voices were the new way of life.

Colton didn't want to let go of his girls. At this moment, he thanked God for life's greatest blessing—the love of a family. In the darkness, the Rymans didn't say a word for several minutes. Their embrace said it all. Family was their circle of strength, founded on faith, joined in love. They would endure together—forever.

"Guys, there's something you have to see," said Colton, rubbing the backs of his girls before heading to the kitchen door leading to the driveway. "It's phenomenal."

He led them outside onto the brick-paver driveway. The popping of the Wagoneer's motor cooling down blended in with the crickets' orchestra and were the only sounds heard.

Wisps of blue and green floated across the dark sky. As the electrically charged particles from the sun collided with Earth's atmosphere, the most common auroral color, a pale greenish-yellow, filled the sky. As nitrogen particles collided, blues were introduced, providing an entrancing, magical display for the world to see.

"Daddy, this is amazing," marveled Alex, who slowly walked in circles, attempting to take it all in. "I've been looking at pictures online, but to see the northern lights is—"

BOOM! BOOM!

CRACKLE, CRACKLE, CRACKLE!

BOOM!

An explosion followed by rapid snaps sounding similar to fireworks or sparklers ripped through the tranquility. The South Davidson Substation, five miles to their west, had just erupted into flames as the incredible surge of energy from the geomagnetic storm overwhelmed its protective relay systems. These systems were designed to trip certain breakers when a fault was detected, like a significant surge in energy. The battery backup system failed, the substation infrastructure was compromised, and the substation became a raging inferno.

The Rymans instinctively ran into their front yard to see the ball of fire gradually rise above Belle Meade Country Club. Colton looked down the hill of their front yard and saw their neighbors gathered on the sidewalk, looking towards the colorful sky. They also appeared to be distracted by the sound.

Then Colton heard it. It was hissing at first and gradually grew louder to a hum.

BUZZZZZZ!

The mysterious noise grew in intensity as it progressed into an ominous crackling in the distance. Out of the corner of his eye, Colton was the first to see the flashes of light rapidly coming towards them. He tried to process the correlation between sight and sound. It was beyond his comprehension, and then he realized what was happening.

"Hey!" Colton shouted as he ran down the hill to the center of his yard. "Run! Run! Get away from the street!"

His neighbors, the O'Malleys, looked back at him, dumbfounded. Their feet weren't moving. Colton waved his arms and yelled once again before he slipped and lost his footing in the wet, dewy grass. He rolled onto his stomach and covered his head as he saw the unimaginable.

A fireball was blazing along the power lines from the substation. Fueled by the electrical surge, it strengthened and then obliterated the transformer at the top of the power pole across the road.

Sparks, fire, and debris rained down upon the people on the sidewalk. The blast was emanating an extreme amount of heat, which caused the trees to erupt spontaneously into an inferno. Mr. O'Malley, his shirt on fire, was frantically rolling around on the wet grass to put out the flames. Screams filled the air as burning tree branches fell to the ground.

As the transformer finally gave way, the red-hot, glowing power lines broke free and fell to the sidewalk, dancing like rattlesnakes that had lost their heads, but not their will to strike. Mrs. O'Malley was electrocuted, dying instantly. Her husband, still smoldering from the burns, scrambled through the wet grass towards her to help and was electrocuted from the conductivity.

The fireball, meanwhile, roared toward Forest Hills, where the Nashville Electric Service substation suffered a similar fate. In its wake, fires were set along Harding Place all the way to Interstate 65.

Madison and Alex rushed to Colton's side. "Colton!" exclaimed Madison. "Are you okay?"

"Daddy!" cried Alex as she also slipped and fell, rolling onto her father.

They shielded their faces from the intense heat generated by the burning oils spilled by the older transformers. Colton helped Alex to her feet and led them back towards the house. His face was burning as if he had fallen asleep under a heat lamp.

"Alex, grab some buckets from the pool house," instructed Colton. Alex took off, and he turned his attention to his wife, who had a frightened look on her face. "Madison, I need you to open the garage and pull the Wagoneer inside. The keys are in it. Close the garage door behind you. You'll have to pull the red string to unlatch it."

She nodded. "Are you sure you're okay?"

"I am. Now hurry, honey. Nobody can know about our truck, okay."

Madison took off up the hill and crossed paths with Alex, who had returned with two five-gallon pails that had been used for pool chemicals.

"Are these the ones, Daddy?"

"Yes, baby. We have to help put out the fires," replied Colton.

"Won't the fire trucks come and do it?" she asked.

"I don't know, Alex. I don't think so. Let's go."

Colton and Alex shielded their faces as they took a wide berth around the smoldering transformer. The fire had died out somewhat, but the fallen tree branches were still burning. With the recent one-hundred-degree heat and the lack of rainfall, Colton didn't want the fire to get out of control.

"Oh my God, Dad," shouted Alex as she paused near the charred bodies of their neighbors. She covered her face as the stench from the burning bodies permeated the air.

"Don't look, Alex," said Colton as he grabbed her arm and pulled her with him. "There's nothing we can do for them right now."

The next-door neighbor stood with a water hose in the middle of the O'Malleys' yard. Colton and Alex ran past him as he mumbled, "It won't work. There's no water."

"Come with us," yelled Colton as he ran through the side gate to the O'Malleys' backyard pool. They scooped up as much water as they could carry and returned to douse the flames.

"What can we do?" asked Rusty Kaplan. He and his wife, Karen, were the Rymans' immediate neighbors on the right.

"Hey, Rusty," Colton greeted him. "You and Karen try to find some buckets in the greenhouse over there. We'll start with these."

A couple of other neighbors joined in while others stood off in the distance, doing nothing. It took thirty minutes for Colton and his neighbors to put out the flames. Sadly, through it all, the O'Malleys lay on their front lawn, dead and forgotten. Colton retrieved a tarp and some cinder blocks from their backyard. He would come back in the morning to bury them—the first of several he would bury in the coming days.

CHAPTER 2

DAY ONE
12:30 a.m., September 9
Ryman Residence
Belle Meade, Tennessee

Colton collapsed in the lawn chair and stared at the wondrous sky. How could something so amazing and beautiful wreak havoc like this? Madison brought him a Red Bull. He smiled up at her and gently reached for her hand.

"Do you think I need the caffeine?" he asked as he popped the top.

"No, love. Just considered it a reward for a job well done. There aren't many of these left, you know."

Colton relaxed somewhat and studied Alex as she retrieved a couple more citronella candles to provide some protection against the mosquitos. The aurora created was so bright, Colton could make out the words on his Red Bull can. He expected the northern lights would last for days.

Alex joined her parents and sat in the chair next to them, letting out a sigh.

"I was right," said Alex.

She stared upward and took it all in. She had been a real soldier as a member of the fire brigade. Her maturity amazed Colton.

"Yes, you were," replied Madison as she continued to admire the aurora.

The Rymans shared the details of their day with one another into the early hours of the morning. As Colton learned of their exploits, he was astonished at the strength and determination of the Ryman women. Any concerns about their ability or desire to survive he might have entertained on the long drive from Dallas were set aside. They'd both be assets in the struggles the family faced in the coming days and weeks.

After they'd talked, Colton needed to speak to Madison about Alex and their uncertain future. Alex was mature for her age, but some matters needed to be discussed between parents before bringing their child into the conversation.

"It's getting late, guys, and I have a few things to do like unload the Suburban and make sure we're secure for the evening," started Colton. He stood up and stretched his legs, rolling his shoulders to work out the stiffness. Between the full-day car ride, the slide down the hill, and the all-hands-on-deck fire brigade, his nearly forty body was feeling the effects already. Colton regretted not being in better shape. He was not an ex-military action hero or a mild-mannered salesman turned Rambo. He would have to adapt, and quickly.

"We're gonna need to sleep in shifts. Until they can restore power, we'll have to keep a vigilant eye. After the things we experienced today, our safety is the first order of business."

"Daddy, the power's not coming back on," interrupted Alex. "It may be like this for years."

"We don't know that, honey," interjected Madison. "I'm sure the government has a plan for something like this. Surely they anticipated—"

"No, Mom, they don't have a plan. They were warned. They've known for longer than I've been alive that this could happen. The government didn't want to spend the money. They're stupid."

"Okay, okay," said Colton, stopping the conversation as he settled back into his chair. "We can talk about the whys and wherefores more tomorrow. For now, the most important thing is sleeping in shifts. Alex, you're first to get some shut-eye. Come give me a kiss, and hit the hay."

"All right, Daddy." She succumbed to her father's orders. She leaned down and gave him a peck on the cheek. "I love you. I love you too, Mom." She gave Madison a hug and entered the dark living room through the French doors. A loud clang, followed by an *oh crap*, indicated Alex had stumbled over Madison's Faraday cages in the living room.

Colton chuckled. "She'll be all right. This powerless world will take some gettin' used to."

Madison was quiet for a moment, which concerned Colton. As the neighbors hustled to put out the fire, Madison had viewed the scene across the street. She had stared at the O'Malleys' charred remains for several minutes until Colton could cover them. He was concerned about Madison's emotional detachment. Colton and his wife had overcome hurdles in the past, but nobody in America had ever faced the prospect of losing all of their modern conveniences as they were thrust back into the nineteenth century.

"Maddie, what're you thinking?" asked Colton, trying to bring her out of her shell.

Madison let out a deep breath and asked, "What do you *really* think all of this means?"

Colton looked up as a flickering candle in Alex's bedroom window caught his eye. He glanced around their backyard and realized no other homes were in view, but he made a mental note to talk with the girls about avoiding light in the evening hours. He didn't want to draw unnecessary attention to their home from passersby.

Colton reached for his wife's hand and held it. It was clammy and sweaty. He quickly realized Madison was wrought with anxiety. He needed to reassure her while not giving her a false sense of hope. If she was experiencing the first stages of shock or depression, Colton would have to tread lightly.

"I listened to news reports all the way home today," started Colton. "There were experts from all across the spectrum, including scientists, politicians, and even survivalists. Maddie, you know how the news sensationalizes things. They create this huge dramatic situation so you'll stay glued to their network. The bigger the crisis, the fatter the ratings."

"I know, I saw it too," said Madison. "When Alex first brought this to my attention, I disregarded the threat and passed it off as a teenager's fabricated drama. But as I learned more, I came to the realization the threat is real. I wish I'd done more." She began to cry, squeezing his hand tighter.

Colton sat up onto the edge of the lawn chair and faced his distraught wife. He rubbed her arm and shoulders and tried to calm her.

"Honey, what you and Alex did for this family today will probably save our lives. I am so proud of you." He gently wiped her tears from her bruised face.

"I could've done more." She sobbed.

Colton let out a nervous laugh. "Like what? Cleaning out the grocery store single-handedly wasn't enough? You ran over a KIA, for the love of Pete!"

Madison stopped sobbing, but the tears still streamed as she laughed. Colton kissed her cheek and wiped her tears once again.

"You know what I mean," she said.

"Listen to me, darling. Our family is safe, and we're together at home, as it should be. I don't know what we'll face, exactly, but we'll face it together."

Madison nodded. "I'm okay. I feel better."

"Promise?"

"Yes, promise," she replied. "Now, seriously, I'll hitch up my big-girl panties and do what I have to do. Oddly, I didn't hesitate today when it was just Alex and me. Now that you're home, as weird as it sounds, I feel like I've turned over the job of protector to you. Now look at me. I'm a ball of blubbering mush." They both started laughing.

"Very funny," said Colton. "I'm trying to visualize blubbering mush, and it ain't you, love."

Madison nodded and sat up in her chair. She finished off Colton's Red Bull and smiled. "Okay, seriously. Gimme the straight poop. Don't sugarcoat it, 'cause I'll know. We've got our work cut out, don't we?"

Colton relaxed considerably. This was the Madison he married and who he counted on as an equal member of Team Ryman. He decided to give her his relatively uninformed opinion.

"If the blackout lasts longer than a few days, the vast majority of the population will be ill-equipped to deal with the shock to their normal modern-day lives. They won't have water or sufficient food to last long. Mentally, most people are weak. They're not self-reliant. The unprepared will look to the government for help, and when that doesn't materialize, they'll look around, seeking the next best alternative."

"People like us," added Madison.

"Exactly. I feel bad that I never anticipated anything of this magnitude. The warning signs were there. Heck, our country has been threatened by a nuclear EMP attack from China, Russia, North Korea and Iran daily. I guess I just never thought it could happen to us."

"Don't feel bad," said Madison. "I'm at home all day, usually with the news playing in the background. I was aware, probably more so than you. I chose to ignore the warnings."

Colton stood up to stretch again and walked around the perimeter of their pool. He peered through the trees to see if he could see any evidence of light in other homes. The homes were pitch black.

"Our world is much smaller now," started Colton. "In the past, we were capable of flying at high speeds from point A to point B. There were no boundaries, including the ability to travel through space. Now, streets, neighborhoods, and towns are our universe. For most people, their world will only be as big as they're capable of reaching on foot or a bicycle."

"What happens when this reality sets in?" asked Madison.

"For a couple of days, our neighbors will hold out hope for a rescue, so to speak," started Colton. "We'll know more about their attitudes as we begin to interact with them over the coming days. These will be difficult times because people won't know where to turn."

Colton pulled the cell phone out of his pocket and showed it to Madison. He tried to power it on, but it was dead.

"I get it," she said. "People crave information, and they won't have a means to get it. They're used to picking up the phone and calling the police or the air-conditioning repairman or a doctor or whatever. All of that is gone now."

"Well, especially the police part," said Colton. "This was the reason I wanted Alex to go to bed. Madison, our fellow man is the most dangerous living creature on the planet. My grandfather taught me to never underestimate the depravity of man. I believe evil will be on full display."

Madison rose to join him. She gave him a hug and reassuring smile. He was amazed how well she knew him. Colton was genuinely concerned about their ability to protect themselves. It was just the three of them.

He continued. "Granddaddy used to talk about his days in World War Two. He said in any survival situation, think about what can most likely kill you and protect against that first. Mark that off your checklist, and then consider the next threat, and so on."

"Makes sense," said Madison. "Have you thought about it?"

"I have," he replied. "Human nature encouraged me to rush around here in a panic, trying to protect our home all at once. We need to think this through logically because our supplies and resources are limited. We have to secure our home first, and that will be the first order of business tomorrow."

"Okay," said Madison. "I have some things I picked up today that will be useful."

Early in the day, Colton came to the realization that an America without power was no different than a third world country. A new range of threats would become a part of their everyday lives.

"Great," started Colton. He picked up the leaf skimmer for the pool and stirred the stagnant water. "Water is life. If we become dehydrated, we'll die. If we drink unpurified water, we'll get dysentery, which will cause diarrhea and nausea. This will exacerbate the dehydration process, and we'll die sooner."

"Nicely put." Madison laughed.

"Thanks," said Colton. "You said don't hold back."

"Yeah, well, I thought about that today too," said Madison

proudly. "Our fresh water is pumped to us from Metro's water plants. If the power is out, the pumps won't work. I bought a few things at the sporting goods store that will help, but I don't know for how long."

"In addition to dysentery, starvation kills people in undeveloped nations as well," added Colton. "Our bodies will break down without proper nutrition. We'll need the energy to defend ourselves from others."

Madison approached him and patted his slightly enlarging, soft, middle-aged belly. "I've got you covered there too, husband. You'll be glad I ran over the KIA."

Colton sat on the retaining wall holding up the hill behind their home. He still wore his suit pants, complete with bloody holes in the knees and newly introduced grass stains. He repeated his grandfather's words. "Never underestimate the depravity of man. We have to try to stay under the radar. Our best defense is to avoid the fight altogether. If we lie low and don't draw attention to ourselves, maybe we can avoid conflicts."

Madison sat next to him and put her arm around his waist. "I guess it all depends on what is going on around us. Tomorrow, we'll figure it out."

"Yup," said Colton. "Please go get some rest. I need to unpack your truck and store that stuff out of sight, and honestly, I need to enjoy this quiet time to think all of this through. Cool?"

"Cool," replied Madison. "I'm so glad you're home safe. I don't care about what's ahead. I'm thankful for what I have right at this moment."

"I love you, Maddie," said Colton as he kissed his wife good night.

CHAPTER 3

DAY ONE
3:00 a.m., September 9
ALMA
Atacama, Chile

Dr. Andrea Stanford sat alone in front of the triple-panel monitors vacated by her associate Deb Daniels. Daniels, like several other members of the JAO Team, was sent home to seek shelter during the second incoming G5 geomagnetic storm. Only her assistant Jose and a skeleton maintenance crew remained.

Over the past several decades, Earth's ozone layer in the atmosphere, which provided a blanket of protection from the sun's damaging rays, had been thinning. As a result, the sun's radiation could reach the earth more easily, resulting in an increase in the incidence of skin cancers.

Earth's magnetosphere was under assault. The X58 solar flare punched the planet in the gut, and the trailing blast of heat energy from the coronal mass ejection knocked Mother Earth to her knees. Dr. Stanford rubbed her temples and studied the data. The knockout blow from the celestial body that gave us life wasn't going to be a sucker punch. It wasn't a left hook to the blind side. This second massive geomagnetic storm was going to hit the Earth square in the jaw at a time when its defensives were at its weakest.

Although ALMA was located fairly close to the equator, which protected its equipment from the solar electromagnetic pulse, its eight-thousand-foot altitude and corresponding thin atmosphere resulted in a deadly combination for this second wave of ultraviolet radiation. The UV levels were twenty percent higher than at sea level, and when coupled with the proximity to the equator, the risk of permanent damage to the eyes, in the form of cataracts, and the skin, in the form of melanoma, was high.

Dr. Stanford was exhausted. She'd just sent a message to NORAD at Cheyenne Mountain. The data was preliminary, but her conclusions were solid. A series of solar storms were likely to strike the planet forty-eight hours after the first one.

NASA dubbed yesterday's space weather event—both the X58-flare and the G5 geomagnetic storm—the *Impactor*. Impactor was the strongest solar storm known to man, easily surpassing the strength and intensity of the widely known Carrington Event of 1859.

In 2014, a team of physicists studied the Carrington Event and every major solar storm since the early twentieth century. By extrapolating the frequency of ordinary solar storms and comparing the data to the instances of extreme storms, the physicists calculated the odds of a Carrington-level storm to be twelve percent.

Having been born in Las Vegas, the gambling mecca of the world, Dr. Stanford knew those odds weren't very good. But when you considered the devastating impact a geomagnetic storm of this magnitude would have on the earth's critical infrastructure, the odds were actually high. It was a sobering figure.

AR3222 had erupted. It hadn't just produced the largest coronal mass ejection on record, but another and another. Impactor was just the beginning. It plowed a road through space, allowing the solar winds to soar across the void unimpeded.

AR3222 was alive, fertile, and spawning offspring. Impactor cleared the way for the stork to drop the babies to Earth—in a hurry.

CHAPTER 4

DAY ONE
4:00 a.m., September 9
Ryman Residence
Belle Meade, Tennessee

Colton fumbled his way through the darkness and found a change of clothes in the laundry room. He disposed of his ruined suit pants in the kitchen trash can. Exiting through the kitchen door allowed him to take a breath of fresh air, as the interior of the home was already filling up with stale hot air due to the lack of circulation from the HVAC system.

This simple process, which he would take for granted on an ordinary day, immediately raised his awareness of how dire this situation was. Without power, how would they wash their clothes? Where would they dispose of garbage? How would they heat their home in the dead of winter? These were all everyday activities that, had he planned ahead, he could have prepared for.

Instead of a large box of powdered laundry detergent, they would've purchased the liquid type, which was easily dissolved. Colton wished he had boxfuls of thick lawn and leaf bags for his garbage instead of the thin white kitchen style. A wood-burning fireplace would've been a much better option than the *clean, energy-efficient* natural gas burner he was convinced to install by the Piedmont Gas contractor.

Work with what you've got, Colton's dad would always say. With that in mind, he continued setting up their home for life with no electricity. As tempting as it was to scramble around in a frenzy and do everything before sunrise, Colton suppressed his adrenaline, stress, and fear to allow himself the opportunity to assess their home.

He walked onto the sidewalk leading to their front door and stood in the midst of the red Double Knock Out roses. His lawn was impeccable, and its steep slope provided a deterrent to people or vehicles approaching from the street. He studied the driveway and decided to block it with the Suburban.

Colton had no intention of pulling the Jeep Wagoneer out of the garage. He considered it their most valuable asset. If it was necessary to go, they probably wouldn't be coming back. He unpacked the Suburban and emptied out all of the compartments. Simple things like pens, paper, and a flashlight key ring all had value now. He even removed the tire-changing kit from the trunk. *Take nothing for granted.*

After he secured the generator and the propane tanks in the garage, he set about maneuvering the Suburban down the driveway. He placed the truck in neutral and muscled the steering wheel in the proper direction. *He'd miss power steering.* Colton began to push, and then he leaped into the driver's seat just as the Suburban began rolling on its own.

As it picked up speed rolling down the sloped driveway, Colton began to question the plan. The power brakes didn't work, and the steering was difficult to control. He held on.

The passenger side of the truck careened into the flower bed and elevated itself on top of the decorative retaining wall. But it stopped nonetheless and blocked the entrance to their driveway. *Epic fail*, or *mission accomplished*, depending on how you looked at it.

Colton walked into the middle of Harding Place. At this hour, the streets would normally be quiet, but the decorative street lanterns would be shining brightly. Tonight, the aurora was painted on a pitch black canvas sky. It allowed him to stop and consider his priorities. Standing within a few feet of the O'Malleys' dead bodies reminded him that he'd have to deal with them before sunrise. The hundred-degree heat of the day would make disposing of their corpses very unpleasant.

He quietly walked up and down the street for several minutes as he recalled the neighbors watching as he frantically worked to douse the fire hours ago. Why didn't they pitch in and help? With that in mind, he considered—who could he count on?

On the right side of the Rymans' home lived Rusty and Karen Kaplan. They had been his neighbors for six years and were scheduled to come over this evening for the party. Rusty was the local Chevy dealer who sold them the Suburban. Colton would have to tell him about his experience with the Corvette—but not about the trade. Karen taught preschool at the nearby Methodist Church. They were good people and Colton thought he could count on them.

Drs. Bill and Diane Young lived on the left side of the Ryman home. Both psychiatrists, Colton was sure they previously mocked all of their clients who held delusional fantasies of a post-apocalyptic world. He'd have to ask them about that. The Youngs were antigun, pro-abortion, Suburu-drivin' liberals who tucked themselves into bed with the comfort of knowing their government would rescue them at first light. While their politics were the opposite of Colton's, they weren't a threat to his family's safety.

Finally, an elderly woman, Mrs. Alma Abercrombie, lived on the other side of the Youngs. She was a sweet lady whose husband, a Vietnam War veteran, died back in the spring. Other than the usual wave and exchange of pleasantries on the sidewalk, Colton had very little interaction with her. He made a mental note to check up on her soon.

Colton focused his attention on the homes of Harding Place and some of their features. The O'Malleys had a greenhouse and a pool—*food and water.* There were cable television repairs going on under the road just past the Abercrombie home—*tools and hardware.* Across the street from an abandoned Comcast repair van, a house was being renovated—*lumber and building materials.*

Then he focused his attention on his own place. Their pool held over twenty thousand gallons of water, but it was stagnant. With no operable pool pump, it wouldn't take long for algae bloom and mosquitos to take over. He had granulated pool shock for his floating chlorinator, but that would quickly run out. They'd have to work pool maintenance into their routine.

If they brushed twice a day—*per his dentist's instructions*, Colton laughed to himself—and immediately removed debris from the pool, which was a likely source of bacteria and algae, the Rymans would have an unlimited source of water. Proper hygiene was critical.

Colton imagined the government would find a way to get power to area hospitals, but getting there was not an option for most. Pharmacies were closed down and most likely the first place looted. He was sure the drug addicts of Metro Davidson County trashed the place like kids in a candy store, looking for narcotics. If it were up to him, Colton would be picking up the scraps off the floor—namely, antibiotics. He wondered if the Fish Mox Alex used in her aquarium would be a decent substitute.

As he made his way back up the hill to his house, a slight southern breeze brought the smell of burnt flesh to his nostrils, reminding him that he needed to bury the O'Malleys. As he returned from their greenhouse with a shovel, Colton contemplated death.

Experiencing someone's death could be a frightening event, and the fear of dying was universal. We passed by hospitals, funeral homes, and hospices daily, allowing them to do the dirty work of dealing with death and the dying. Our cemeteries were expertly hidden behind fences, walls, and hedgerows. Most of us were unwilling to acknowledge what lay behind those visual barriers.

In a post-apocalyptic world, we could no longer hide from death, and most of us would not be prepared to face the probability that ninety percent of Americans would die as a result of this catastrophe. Colton's lesson in dealing with the dead began now.

He removed the cinder blocks and tarp covering the O'Malleys' bodies. Colton saw that Mr. O'Malley's last, dying effort was to grasp his wife's charred hand. It was a loving act that allowed the O'Malleys one brief touch before their demise. It broke Colton's heart.

Colton leaned on the shovel and allowed himself to cry as he prayed for their souls. The O'Malleys were missionaries once and very active in their Catholic church. They were good people and didn't deserve this.

He wanted to bury them in the privacy and serenity of their

backyard. The O'Malleys obviously enjoyed gardening, and the backyard setting would've been ideal. However, their bodies wouldn't survive the move. He opted instead for a raised planter bed that contained a variety of plants. Colton set about digging out the plants and carefully placing them to the side. He removed the mulch and the soft topsoil beneath.

For protection, Colton put on some gardening gloves and wrapped a bandana around his face that he found in their greenhouse. He positioned the bodies onto the tarp and pulled them to the shallow grave. Thirty minutes later, they were properly tucked in their resting place until they would return to dust in about fifteen years. Colton carefully transplanted the plant material, and the sounds of barking dogs reminded him to place the available concrete pavers on top of their graves.

His gravedigger duties over, Colton crossed the street to his home as the sun rose in the east over Forest Hills. It was only the beginning of day one.

CHAPTER 5

DAY ONE
Noon, September 9
Ryman Residence
Belle Meade, Tennessee

Colton woke up refreshed. Before going to bed, he had washed up outside, using two buckets of pool water and Ivory soap, which floated on the top of the soap bucket. It was a new experience for him to stand naked in the backyard, pouring buckets of water over his head at sunrise. He felt like a hippie.

After six hours of hard sleep, he came downstairs and found all of the windows open and a slight breeze causing the window sheers to billow. If he didn't know better, it was just another fall day, albeit a hot one. He found Alex on the couch, fiddling with a portable radio.

"Good morning, Allie-Cat," he said cheerfully as he gave his daughter a peck on the cheek.

"Hey, Daddy," she responded, not admonishing him for the cutesy reference.

"Whatcha got there?" he asked, looking over her shoulder.

"It's a hand-crank radio Mom bought yesterday. It's pretty cool because it doesn't need electricity."

"Have you picked up any stations?"

"Not really," she replied. "I thought maybe there would be an emergency alert or something. So far, all I can muster is a faint signal from some Spanish-speaking station. The only words I understand are *hola* and *del sol*. They talk a whole lot faster than the teacher in my Spanish One class."

"That's a start. What's for breakfast?"

"Ha-ha, very funny, Daddy," she responded dryly. "Mom fixed a brunch consisting of breakfast casserole, biscuits and gravy, and eggs benedict with hollandaise sauce—your choice."

"Good point." He chuckled.

"I had a Pop-Tart out of the pantry. Mom bought the variety pack yesterday, but save the blueberry for me, okay?"

"Okay, honey," replied Colton. He walked into the kitchen and back around through the dining room, seeing the extent of Madison's shopping efforts for the first time. He was impressed. "Speaking of your mom, where is she, anyway?"

Alex set the radio on the coffee table and assumed a prone position on the couch. Colton hadn't assigned daily chores yet, but staring at the ceiling in the middle of the day wouldn't be one of them. He'd address it in a moment.

"She was on the front steps, but I think I heard her talking with the neighbors next door," replied Alex, getting settled in.

"Which ones?" asked Colton as he made his way to the front door.

"The Youngs."

Colton opened the door and stepped into the searing heat. It was approaching the mid-nineties today—*another scorcher*, as Ron Howes, the recently retired NewsChannel 5 meteorologist, would say. Madison was returning from her chat and ran to Colton when she saw him.

"I missed you," she whispered in his ear as they hugged. In that moment, the two quietly realized how precious their lives were together, and they would never take for granted the opportunity to hold one another.

"I missed you more," said Colton as he glanced at the graves of the O'Malleys.

Madison caught him looking down the hill toward the road. "You buried them this morning."

"I did. Maddie, they were holding hands when they died. It was heart-wrenching." Colton's eyes began to well up with tears. It was Madison's turn to comfort her husband.

"You're a good man, Colton, and I love you. When it's our time to go, I want us to hold hands too."

Colton wiped his tears and held Madison tight. He vowed to protect his family, and that was the first item on today's agenda.

"How are Dr. and Dr. Young? Did they put you on the couch and ask *how does this make you feel?*"

"Zip it, mister," Madison replied, adding a slug to Colton's sore shoulder muscles. "They were very nice and supportive. They offered to help us with anything we needed although they admittedly have very little food in the house. Diane said they almost always eat out."

Colton looked toward their home and saw them entering the front door. They exchanged friendly waves. "Did they ask any questions about us?"

"Like what?"

"I don't know. I mean, like, *how much food do you have*, for example."

"No," replied Madison. "We had a friendly chat, and they weren't wearing their psychobabble hats today. They're convinced this will only last a few days and the President will have the nation back on track soon. Their biggest concern was whether patients would get their prescribed antidepressant medications."

"Good. We need to keep our food and supplies to ourselves."

"I agree," interjected Madison. "The Youngs are concerned about safety. They were coming home yesterday as the attempted carjacking took place on Belle Meade Boulevard. They saw the crashed vehicle and the men running up the hill toward Iroquois. Do you think the carjackers are still around?"

"Possibly," replied Colton. "We learned yesterday that the biggest threat we face is the unexpected. I've given this some thought, and I have a plan."

"It's a little cooler inside, should we go in?" asked Madison.

"Yeah, and also," started Colton as they made their way up the steps to the front door, "we need to establish a routine today, and Alex needs to be a part of it."

Madison led the way to the living room as Colton hoisted Alex's legs up and playfully swung her around.

"Hey!" she objected. "I was thinking about a little *siesta.* See, I'm learning Spanish already. Does this mean I can homeschool now?"

"Ha-ha, missy." Madison laughed. "We'll talk about school and studies later. Kids in the eighteen hundreds had to go to school too, you know."

"Mom, girls my age in the eighteen hundreds were married and pregnant already," Alex shot back. Colton shuddered at the thought.

"She's got a point, Maddie." Colton laughed.

"Forget it," said Madison with her arms folded defiantly. "We've got a shotgun, and I bought shells. I have no problem practicing using *live boys* as targets!"

Everyone laughed as Colton sat up in his seat and wiped the sweat off his forehead. He had to tell the girls the reality of the threats they faced from their fellow man. One mistake, one mental lapse resulting in their guards being let down, could be deadly.

In the future, conversations like this without one set of eyes on the home's perimeter wouldn't take place. It was daytime of the first day. Surely the bad guys wouldn't attack this soon after the power grid collapsed.

"It's very important that we talk about security," started Colton.

"Did Mom show you our toy guns?" asked Alex.

"I saw them and they're amazingly realistic," replied Colton. "I'm glad that you mentioned them. I want us to carry one of the faux handguns in our waistband anytime we're in the presence of our neighbors. I want them to know that we're armed. I hope it will act as a deterrent to prevent them from trying something stupid."

"Like what?" asked Alex.

"I don't know how folks will react to this catastrophe," started Colton as he relaxed back into his chair. "I suspect it'll go something like this. For the first couple of days, the public will bond together and help one another. They'll expect the situation to resolve itself quickly, and most will be in a compassionate mind-set. I'm really not concerned about our safety the first couple of days."

"I feel a *but* coming," interrupted Madison.

"*But*, once help doesn't arrive and the power remains off, the public will become more aware of the severity of the situation. At that point, depression and desperation will set in."

"When?" asked Alex.

"I don't know. An extensive grid-down scenario, if that's what we're facing, is new to all of us. The Youngs might know how the public will react. I don't. The power could be out for a week. It could be dark for three or four days. You guys experienced firsthand how the public reacted at the mere suggestion of a problem."

"Here's what I learned from yesterday," added Madison. "It's one thing for our neighbors to endure a temporary power outage due to a bad storm. I can only imagine what they'll be like when they figure out this could last for months or years."

"Exactly," said Colton. "We have to establish some security measures, a routine, and some ground rules."

"Great, rules," moaned Alex. She leaned back and hugged a pillow.

"Yes, dear, rules," said Colton. "They're not like you think. Rule number one is *trust no one.* No exceptions unless we discuss it as a family. As we get deeper into this catastrophe, our friends and neighbors will become potentially hostile and will use anything they learn about our situation to harm us. Remember, *loose lips sink ships*, so trust no one—very important."

"Got it," said Alex. "What's rule number two?"

"Maintain mental discipline and a level head under pressure," replied Colton. "You guys did a great job of that last night when the Wrens came over unexpectedly. I'm sure that conversation is not over. Regardless, it would've been easy for Mom to give them a good blasting, but she didn't. You also managed to shield all of our food supplies from their view. Good work."

"Thanks," said Madison, smiling. "Do you think they'll be back?"

"Count on it," replied Colton. "This leads me to the third rule. We must continually be aware of our surroundings. If we maintain a heightened state of awareness by keeping an eye on our yard and things going on up and down our street, we'll be able to react quickly to a potential threat."

"Paranoid, but not quite," added Madison.

"Yes," said Colton. "Above all, every decision that's made is going to be in the best interest of this family. Our choices may seem harsh or crass at times, but the same standard will always apply. *What will keep us alive?*"

Alex hung her head and appeared to be dejected. She picked up the radio and mindlessly fiddled with the dials. Colton looked at Madison, who noticed it as well. She went over to their daughter and sat on the coffee table across from her. She took the radio out of her hands like she would take a toy from a dejected child. Madison knew just what to say.

"Alex, listen to me," started Madison as she wiped a tear away from Alex's cheek. "Just because it's the end of the world as we know it doesn't mean it's the end of the world."

Chapter 6

DAY ONE
4:00 p.m., September 9
Ryman Residence
Belle Meade, Tennessee

"The most important thing for us to remember is that we want to give people the appearance that we'll put up a fight," said Colton as he walked around the outside of the house with Madison and Alex.

Alex started laughing as she pointed at the Suburban. "They'll certainly be afraid of your driving, Daddy."

"That is scary looking," said Madison. "Maybe we should shoot it full of bullets and paint on the side—*looters beware*!" Colton actually thought about this for a minute. *Not a bad idea. If we catch a looter, maybe we should string them up by their toes and hang them from one of the oak trees.*

"At some point in time," started Colton, stopping in the middle of the front yard, "we'll have to deal with people who want to take what we have. The strong will band together and prey on the weak. Rather than clashing with a bunch of armed thugs, the idea is to make them move on to easier targets."

Madison put her hands on her hips and surveyed the burnt landscape across the street. She looked up and down and was still digesting the lack of activity. Several neighbors to their east had congregated in the middle of the road for a cookout. *Strange times.*

Colton continued. "We're not living in some fictional reality with stockpiles of weapons and ammo. Our reality consists of a family with one shotgun that none of us have fired. We have several dozen shells of various types, only one of which I can identify—birdshot."

"For birds, right?" asked Alex.

"Ding, ding, ding. We have a winner," said Colton. "I'm guessin' buckshot is for deer. Slugs must be for, um, sluggin' it out. Who knows?"

"There's a manual, and we could always ask someone," replied Madison. "I think Rusty has a gun of some kind."

"In the meantime, our goal is deterrence, not defeat," said Colton. "We don't know how to fight, yet. If negotiation is an option, we'll try that first. If that doesn't work, a warning shot will be next. We can't take any chances."

Alex grasped the concept immediately. "It seems to me anybody, including thugs, would find another house to steal from if they're getting shot at, right?"

"I hope so," said Colton. "The idea is to avoid a gun battle and encourage the bad guys to move on to easier targets. There will always be easier targets."

Madison reached down and plucked a rose near the front entry. She handed it to Alex. "I'm worried about our windows. Look how big they are and near the ground. Anyone could easily break them out and climb into the formal living room."

"I've thought about this as well," said Colton. "Tonight, right after dark, Alex and I are going to run and make a couple of stops."

Alex stopped dead in her tracks. "Hold up," she started, raising her hands. "The last time I went on a *run* with one of you guys, Mom and I had to run for our lives." They all laughed.

"Honey, I promise we won't be out long and most likely won't encounter any thugs, or KIAs."

"Very funny," said Madison. "Why do you have to go after dark?"

"I don't want the neighbors watching us enter the yards of other people's homes. There are resources up and down this street that we can take advantage of."

"Like?" questioned Madison.

Colton gestured across the street. "The O'Malleys have a large roll of black landscape fabric in their greenhouse. We'll borrow it to affix to the inside of our lower-floor windows. This will prevent any inside light from escaping. At night, we don't want to become a beacon of opportunity for the bad guys."

"What's the other stop?" asked Alex.

"There's a vacant house being renovated down the street. It's like having our own Home Depot. We'll find some wood and other materials to board up the windows. That should at least slow down intruders and encourage them to look for easier pickin's."

"You've really thought this through," said Madison.

He was sweating profusely again, a family genetic trait. He'd have to remember to stay hydrated. "I have. Listening to all of the EMP and survival experts on the radio yesterday helped. We'll go right after dusk when most of the neighbors are inside and before the bad dudes, if any, hit the streets at midnight—the witching hour."

"Let's go inside, Daddy, and get out of the sun," said Alex, apparently concerned about her father sweltering under the hot sun.

Colton nodded and led them around to the side gate, which entered into the pool area. "One more thing before we go inside. The rear is our most vulnerable part of the property. If I were a burglar, this would be an ideal point of entry."

The Rymans' backyard consisted of the pool house and the pool contained within a short retaining wall structure. A six-foot-tall wooden privacy fence blocked out the surrounding neighbors and connected the house to the other structures. Heading north up an embankment away from the Ryman home was a wooded, heavily landscaped area that would provide any intruder perfect cover as they approached the back of the house. In the dark of the night, a looter could be right on top of them easily without being detected.

Alex recalled a similar situation. "Mom, do you remember last year when some of the neighborhood boys snuck up on me when I was lying out in the sun? They scared me to death."

"Yeah, I remember," replied Madison. "I also remember them running for their lives when you started pelting them with pea gravel."

"I was listening to my iPod, which allowed them to sneak up on me."

Colton interrupted. "Exactly, Alex. You couldn't hear them

coming. We can remedy that. You notice how quiet it is now, right?"

Both of the Ryman women nodded their heads. Colton walked over to the garbage cans and pulled out an empty Red Bull can. He poured some pea gravel in it and gave it a shake.

Rattle, rattle, rattle.

"We'll take some of the fishing line from the gear you found and string it through the pop tops of these Red Bull cans. We'll wind it through the trees to create a trip alarm. I also have some other barriers and booby traps in mind."

Madison took the can from Colton and shook it. "Won't that use up a lot of fishing line?"

"It can. My thought is to create an easy path down the hill for the bad guys."

"What?" asked Alex. "I thought the idea is to make it harder for them to come down the hill."

Colton hopped up on the wall and walked up into the trees about twenty yards. "They have this entire stretch to make their way to the house. I don't think we can block it all, nor can we set trip alarms this far apart." He started spreading the mulch with his feet between two oak trees.

"You look like the guy on HGTV, Daddy," said Alex.

Colton nodded and continued. "We'll create a path that encourages them to enter this six-foot-wide entry point. We'll set up our trip alarms a few yards above this, which will give us time to react. If they come at us in a group, they'll get congested here in a bunch, and we can shoot them all at once. The landscaping and the slope creates a natural spot for them to clump together."

"We'll have to act fast," said Madison. "But knowing this is the most logical part of the yard a burglar would use allows us to focus on it."

"Plus, Alex's bedroom window is right there," said Colton, pointing above their heads. "She'll hear them coming through the woods before they reach the makeshift alarms."

"If I had a gun up there, I could shoot them as they tried to get away," said Alex.

Colton knew they were woefully short of weapons to defend their home. He thought of ways to obtain more guns. Making deals was what came to mind first, but it seemed foolish to trade food, the most valued commodity at the moment. An opportunity would present itself. He was sure of it.

CHAPTER 7

DAY ONE
6:00 p.m. MT, September 9
NORAD
Cheyenne Mountain, Colorado

There were four aircraft available to the President at all times. Air Force One was primarily used during peacetime when the President traveled around the country or overseas. However, one aircraft was always on alert with a full battle staff. Known as the National Airborne Operations Center, or NAOC, it was a militarized Boeing 747 based in Omaha, Nebraska. The NAOC was ready for takeoff on fifteen minutes' notice to be available to the President for commanding the military forces during a crisis.

As nuclear weapons proliferated among the world's superpowers, past administrations began to assess the threats to the United States. Plans were initiated under the Carter administration and fortified by President Ronald Reagan that envisioned a protracted nuclear war lasting days or weeks.

The key concern of the Reagan administration was continuity of government—a series of defined procedures to follow to continue the essential functions of government in case of nuclear war or another catastrophic event.

After the September 11 attacks in 2001, the Bush administration initiated the Continuity of Operations plan for the first time. Nearly one hundred and fifty senior government officials and staff from every federal department were escorted to secure bunkers located on the East Coast at Raven Rock, Pennsylvania, and Berryville, Virginia.

The second time the plan was commenced occurred six hours

before the impact of the coronal mass ejection. The President declared a national state of emergency under National Security Presidential Directive 51—NSPD 51. This executive order, initially executed by President Bush in 2007, gave the President broad powers to ensure the continuity of government in the event of any catastrophic event that resulted in mass casualties, damage or the severe disruption of the nation's critical infrastructure.

The President had the option to remain in the President's Emergency Operations Center—PEOC, located beneath the East Wing of the White House. It served as a secure shelter and communications center during a catastrophic event, an invasion, or nuclear attack. However, after an assessment was made regarding the duration of the repairs necessary to bring back a portion of the nation's power grid, the President opted for Cheyenne Mountain. She said remaining in the cramped PEOC for over a year was unacceptable.

While en route to Colorado Springs, the President signed a series of executive orders pursuant to her authority under NSPD 51. She placed the Department of Homeland Security in firm control of all national policing and recovery efforts. American troops from abroad were recalled to coordinate with the National Guard to maintain order. FEMA's role was expanded to include the takeover of food production and distribution, as well as all medical facilities nationwide.

Aboard the NAOC, she instructed the White House Legal Counsel to prepare the Declaration of Martial Law as being necessary to protect the citizenry and insure continuity of government. The declaration suspended certain provisions of the United States Constitution, including, but not limited to, civil law, civil rights, habeas corpus, and such other and general provisions as might be determined in the national interest by the Office of the President. Specifically, she suspended the entire Bill of Rights.

Now firmly entrenched in the bunker located deep inside the Cheyenne Mountain complex in Colorado Springs, the home of NORAD, the President was receiving her first briefings regarding the conditions throughout the nation.

"Madame President," started Secretary of Homeland Security Blumenthal as he brought the group's attention to a large computer monitor affixed to the wall. He pointed to the two dozen flashing red rings around the twenty largest population centers in America, including New York—the largest—down to the twentieth largest, Memphis. "These areas indicated by the red flashing lights are not controlled at this time. The National Guard has insufficient resources to stem the tide of social unrest. Frankly, Madame President, they could be declared a war zone."

"Why don't you allocate more troops and resources to these cities?" asked the President.

"General," said Blumenthal, directing the question to the chairman of the Joint Chiefs.

"Madame President," replied the general. "The initial recovery plan established by Homeland Security envisioned a joint, collaborative effort between National Guard units and local law enforcement until such point as our troops could be recalled from abroad."

The President leaned forward and addressed the general. "I've recalled the troops. Are you coordinating with local law enforcement?"

"We are attempting to make that effort. However, first responders and the police are in complete disarray. Within these large metropolitan areas, the local political structure has disappeared and so has law enforcement. They've simply abandoned their posts and cannot be located due to the collapse of the communications system. Without those bodies assisting our boots on the ground, it's too dangerous to enter the cities."

"What do you propose, General?" asked the President.

"One of the problems, Madame President …" The general paused to gather his thoughts. "Frankly, the violence is escalating and gradually moving out of the inner city. Even at this early stage of the collapse, gangs are being formed and taking advantage of the absence of control. We can attempt to clamp down on this activity, but it will require a full military effort, something unprecedented on U.S. soil."

The President stared at the map, clasped her hands together, and tapped her index fingers against one another. "I have to do everything I can to eliminate the barriers that stand in the way of our National Guardsmen doing their job to restore order. We cannot allow American citizens to shoot each other to death before we have an opportunity to restore the power and initiate a recovery effort. Secretary Blumenthal, we have to do more to protect our citizens. I want you to begin immediate house-to-house searches of all registered gun owners and start a push for confiscation."

The general interrupted the President. "Madame President, the inner cities are unsafe at this time for our soldiers to conduct these types of searches."

"General, I wasn't finished," admonished the President. "I'm not suggesting we enter the war zone, as Sydney so aptly refers to our inner cities. I want to prevent the violence from spreading into the suburbs and the rural areas. Guns give people a quick, easy and relatively detached method of killing people. If we take away the tools of death, people will still kill others, but it will be far more difficult to accrue the body counts."

The room grew quiet as the general clenched his fist. He never said another word.

"I'll issue the necessary directives," said Secretary Blumenthal.

The White House Chief of Staff spoke next. "The next item on the agenda is the prediction of the second major solar storm scheduled to hit this evening. Scientists at ALMA have provided our skeleton team from the Space Weather Prediction Center the particulars. This next wave of solar plasma will not be nearly as powerful as the first wave, but Earth's magnetic shield is severely weakened at this time."

"What's the bottom line?" gruffed the President, who was still simmering over the general's challenge to her authority.

"Madame President, this second wave will create a severe health risk to the public in the form of increased radiation levels. A warning needs to be issued as soon as possible."

The President slammed her hands on the table. "Great. I'll address the nation. Tell everybody to turn their televisions on tonight at nine. How do I communicate with the country, Syd?"

"I understand your frustration, Madame President," said Secretary Blumenthal. "We can provide them notice via the Emergency Broadcast Network. Naturally, it's not fully operational, but it's something. We can also have the National Guard drive through the streets, making an announcement and posting flyers."

"Great options." She sighed, slamming herself back into the chair. "I don't have enough guardsmen to fight the battles necessary to gain control of our cities. Some of us don't want to go around and collect the guns to prevent people from killing each other. Now, our only option is to send our depleted forces to issue a warning to others and expose themselves to the radiation in the process."

"Madame President, the public will understand we're doing the best we can to—" started Blumenthal until he was interrupted.

"Madame President, there is something else you need to know," announced an aide who rushed into the room, carrying a stack of papers. "We've just received an urgent communication from NOAA. I'm sorry, but the situation is about to get a lot worse."

CHAPTER 8

DAY ONE
7:00 p.m. PT, September 9
Point Loma
San Diego, California

Master Sergeant Eduardo Lopez and his fiancée, Lance Corporal Maria Herrera, sat quietly atop Point Loma, watching the festivities below them. Sounds of laughter surrounding the beachfront bonfires rose into the sky as Californians of all ages celebrated the apocalypse.

This evening was supposed to have been a night of celebration for the betrothed couple. Joined by their families and a hundred of their fellow Marines, the two would've been married at this moment in a beautiful ceremony planned at the Naval Base Point Loma. The Breakers Beach Deck overlooked a vast stretch of the Pacific Ocean with views extending as far south as the historic Hotel Del Coronado. The couple had envisioned exchanging their wedding vows on the deck amid the sounds of waves lapping on the shore. A magnificent sunset like the one they were admiring now would have capped off the perfect day.

Then the news came that the solar storm was coming. The couple had to make a decision. *Do we ignore the warnings, or send our families to safety?* Guests had come from as far away as Mexico City. It would have been impossible for them to return and reach their destination fifteen hundred miles away before the storm was expected to hit.

It was the presidential order for all active-duty personnel to go back to their base that provided the answer. The wedding was canceled, the attendees scrambled for their appointed destinations, and seven members of the couple's families from Mexico crowded into their rented three-bedroom home in the nearby Sunset Cliffs area.

The couple needed to get away and reflect on what might have been and their future. When the power grid collapsed, Lopez and Herrera were torn between their duty to country and obligations to loved ones. Returning to Camp Pendleton meant their families, who spoke little English, would have to fend for themselves. They chose family, and themselves, over the Marines.

They tried not to second-guess their decision, but loyalty to a country that had provided the two dedicated Marines so much tore at their hearts. Their decision was clouded by emotion. Now, their view of San Diego to the east and Tijuana, Mexico, to their south was disappearing into early nightfall.

Their view across San Diego Bay was spectacular as the sun was setting. Looking to the west across the massive Pacific Ocean, the scene was picture perfect, something only God could've created. The question in their mind was similar to millions of others: *How could something so beautiful take away life as we knew it?*

This was just one of many questions the couple would ask themselves as the mood on the beach suddenly changed. The joyous laughter turned to shouts of alarm. In the dimming daylight, the beach partyers could be seen scrambling for higher ground. They were fleeing something.

The collision of the ISS and the Tiandong-1 screamed through Earth's atmosphere at nearly forty thousand miles per hour. When the large, dense hunk of molten metal struck the Pacific Ocean twelve hundred miles to their west, the impact was equivalent to two thousand kilotons of TNT, one hundred times more powerful than the atomic bomb detonated at Hiroshima.

When the asteroid-sized wreckage hit the water, the blast created a crater in the ocean. The displaced water piled up around this crater and formed a ring. As this ring moved out and away from the center of the impact point, the water began to oscillate up and down, forming ringlets that spread outward from the crater. The series of loops and crimps in the water created a tsunami wave train.

Initially, the ringlets produced by the impact were twenty feet high. Fifty miles later, the tsunami wave train doubled in height. Two hundred miles later, it doubled again as it spread in all directions across the Pacific.

Shouts of *help, run*, and *hurry* filled the air. That was when the couple saw the reason for the panic. The ocean was rising. At first, the beaches of the shoreline below slowly disappeared. Lopez and Herrera held hands as they looked up and down the pristine coast, which was gradually swallowed by the sea.

The Marines didn't panic because they were over four hundred feet above the beach. But the ocean rose, and their concerns grew with the rising waters.

The tsunami wave train didn't take the lives of Eddie and Maria that night. The waves lapped up just twenty feet from where they stood at the top of Point Loma. However, the rest of the four-hundred-foot-tall wall of water stretched inland across Mexico and into parts of Arizona. It consumed the entire Southern California region from San Diego to Los Angeles and washed away nearly twenty million people when the water finally receded back into the Pacific twenty hours later.

CHAPTER 9

DAY TWO
10:00 a.m., September 10
Ryman Residence
Belle Meade, Tennessee

The euphoria of Colton's return began to disappear, and reality set in for Madison. Now that he was home, she would try to revert to her preferred role as wife and mom. By the second day, their routines were being established. Colton functioned very well on half a dozen hours of sleep. At sunrise, he'd find his way to bed, where he would wake Madison, who was typically an early riser. Alex tried to adopt the sleeping patterns of a typical teenager during their summer break from school. Working her into a routine might prove difficult.

Madison finished cleaning the pool while she tended to the eggs and bacon. After taking an inventory of their refrigerated items, Madison set up a menu that would last through day four. The meals would be a hodgepodge of frozen dinners and leftovers, but her family would maintain some semblance of nutrition and energy. As their meals turned to the more mundane—beans, rice, and oatmeal—Madison would incorporate the vitamins and nutritional supplements into their daily meal plan.

They made the decision to keep the generator under wraps to avoid drawing attention. Colton wasn't sure how to mask the sound. Running the machine inside the house or even the garage, which was attached to the house through the bonus room, could prove deadly. Noxious carbon monoxide fumes would quickly overtake the stale air inside. Ultimately, the pool house was deemed their only option.

Madison used their newly acquired Camp Chef modular cooking

system that operated on the propane tanks she'd purchased. It burned clean and didn't make any noise. At sixty thousand BTUs, it was very fuel efficient as well. She estimated the available propane she purchased would cook ten days of meals. Propane was high on her wish list, which she'd started after last night's foray into the O'Malleys' backyard and the construction site.

Colton and Alex had run back and forth, finding useful items, sneaking them home, and with each trip, asking Madison to make a note of this or that. With the world at a standstill, a simple item like a garden tool or a box of nails became highly sought after items if you didn't have them already. Madison took on the role of inventory specialist, cataloging the items they had and also high-value items to target. From a safety perspective, she agreed with Colton they had a limited window of opportunity to make these runs. With each passing day, the night would become more dangerous.

"Any luck?" Madison asked Alex as she entered the living room. Alex was assigned the duty of monitoring the radio.

"Yes, actually, there is something," she replied as she took the plate of eggs and bacon. "Wow, thanks, Mom."

"You're welcome, dear. Enjoy these while you can. It may be a while before we see eggs again."

Alex set the radio on the coffee table and turned up the volume to the emergency broadcast she found on a ham radio frequency. The broadcast was a continuous loop recording, but the information provided grabbed Madison's attention. She joined her daughter and listened.

Following a long beep, the broadcast began its two-minute loop. "*We interrupt our programming. Important instructions will follow. Again, this is a National Alert issued by the Department of Homeland Security. The President of the United States has declared a national state of emergency. The text of this declaration can be found posted at local federal buildings and military facilities.*

"Effective immediately, until ended by a presidential decree, the President has declared the following to be in effect. A curfew has been established until further notice. All citizens are required to remain in their homes during the evening hours.

During daytime hours, citizens are encouraged to shelter in place.

"Local law enforcement and the National Guard, in conjunction with the Federal Emergency Management Agency, will be establishing shelters for those displaced from their homes or who are in need of special assistance. Food and water distribution centers will be announced in the coming days. You are encouraged to utilize these services as a last resort only.

"In furtherance of these directives, the President has instructed the National Guard and local law enforcement to break up any unlawful assemblies and confiscate weapons, magazines, and ammunition, such actions determined to be in the best interests of the nation and the safety, health, and general welfare of its citizens.

"Willful violations of the provisions of the President's declaration shall be punishable by imprisonment and asset forfeiture. All American citizens will now fall under the jurisdiction of military tribunals established by this declaration.

The electronic beeping indicated the end of the broadcast and the beginning of the next loop. Alex turned the radio off and set her plate on the table. Madison stared at the radio for a moment. She was glad to hear something, although it was not what she expected. Rather than telling them it was going to be okay and that *our government is there for you*, Madison felt like she was being told to remain under house arrest and instantly felt depressed.

"Whadya think, Mom?" asked Alex, breaking Madison out of her trance.

"I don't know what to think, Alex," replied Madison. "I guess, I mean, I kinda hoped to hear something was being done about the power. Instead, I feel like a prisoner in my home."

Colton rounded the stairs and joined them. "I heard the announcement upstairs. One thing is certain, the government will attempt a response, but they will be overwhelmed and will experience mass defections of their personnel. As society deteriorates, police and National Guardsmen will opt to protect their families rather than fight the looters and thugs in the streets."

"Who'll enforce the law, Daddy?" asked Alex.

"I'm afraid, at least for a while, our nation will have to experience life without the rule of law," replied Colton. He sat in the chair by the fireplace and laced up his tennis shoes. "We'll have to protect ourselves. The laws will still exist, but the process of enforcement and administration will disappear. Our previously publicized and stable laws will no longer act as a deterrent to those using the collapse of the power grid as an opportunity to do bad things."

"What's a military tribunal?" asked Alex.

"The executive branch and the military are probably the only functioning parts of our government right now," replied Colton. "If the police or National Guard arrest somebody, they will be brought before a military court to face justice. What that entails is anybody's guess. Before the collapse, the rule of law governed our nation, as opposed to being governed by arbitrary decisions of government officials. Now, I'm afraid the government will make up the rules as they go."

Madison pointed to the shotgun propped next to Colton by the fireplace. "We only have one gun. Are we giving it up?"

"Not a chance." Colton laughed, picking up the weapon and weighing it in his hands. "Nor will the owners of the other three hundred million weapons in the United States."

"Didn't they do it in New Orleans after Hurricane Katrina?" asked Madison.

"Yes, and it turned out to be a disaster," replied Colton. "They beat up an old lady. They shot another man's dogs. It was a public relations nightmare because the police focused on easy targets—law-abiding citizens. The gun confiscations did nothing to deter the criminals who roamed the French Quarter."

"Should we hide the shotgun?" asked Madison.

"Nope. I'll take my chances with the gun-confiscation directive. I won't take my chances with protecting you guys against the evildoers of the world."

Madison stood and retrieved the radio from the coffee table. Alex tried to stop her. "I want to listen some more, Mom."

"I know you do, Alex," started Madison, who picked it up anyway. "You and I have to cut and staple the landscape fabric to the windows so your dad can nail the boards up today. Besides, when we're not using the electronics, we should keep them stored away in the Faraday cages."

"Why? The storm has already passed," protested Alex.

"I remember the picture of the hole in the Sun you showed me. It looked like it had a few more solar flares in its belly ready to fire at us." Madison tucked the radio away and sealed the lid with the handle of the galvanized trash can. As the lid snapped shut, someone pounded on their front door, startling all of them.

CHAPTER 10

DAY TWO
11:00 a.m., September 10
Ryman Residence
Belle Meade, Tennessee

"Who is it?" shouted Colton through the door as he held the shotgun nervously. There was no answer. He repeated his question, only louder this time. "Who's out there?"

Still no answer. He turned to Madison and Alex, gesturing for them to look out the back door and the kitchen side door. They ran at a low crouch and reached their appointed doors. The sound of clicking dead bolts reminded Colton they weren't following their protocols for keeping entryways locked.

He moved to the living room and peered through the curtains. There wasn't anyone there. Rather than opening the front door to a possible ambush, he left through the kitchen door and moved along the outside wall of the house. Many things went through his mind. *Am I prepared to shoot someone? How does this gun work?*

He immediately chastised himself for not learning the basics of the operation of the Remington shotgun. He took a deep breath and channeled a character on *The Walking Dead* television show. He pumped the fore-end, which generated a loud, metallic sound. *CLACK—CLACK. That would scare me away*, he thought to himself.

Colton, the adrenaline pumping through his body, steadied his nerves to confront the intruder and swung into view. Nobody was there. He pointed the gun in all directions, swinging it towards the garage and back to the front door. Nothing. He relaxed and approached the porch, where a rock was placed on top of a handwritten piece of copy paper.

"Colton?" yelled Madison through the window.

"It's okay," he announced. "You can open the front door."

Madison slowly opened the door, and the girls cautiously peeked out.

"Seriously, y'all," said Colton. "It's safe. We've got mail."

Madison and Alex joined him, nervously looking around the yard. Colton read the note aloud.

"The Harding Place Association of neighbors will be meeting today at noon at the Brileys' former residence located at Trimble and Lynnwood. We encourage everyone to participate as we discuss the power situation. It's signed Shane Wren, President of the HPA."

Colton handed it to Madison, who read it to herself under Alex's probing eyes. He glanced at the cheap Timex watch he'd purchased at T Ricks. They had an hour.

"Where is the smoke coming from?" asked Alex, as she looked up at the black smoke clouds drifting overhead. She instinctively covered her mouth.

"I noticed it this morning as I did my final walk around the house," replied Colton. "It seems to be coming from the west toward Highway 100."

"It stinks."

"Come on, guys, let's get back inside and talk about this meeting," said Colton, leading them into the foyer and locking the door behind them. He took the notice from Madison and examined it again.

"Should we go?" asked Madison.

"You know, just like before the solar flare, I'd rather avoid these things like the plague," said Colton. "I guess, under the circumstances, we should check it out, if for no other reason than to learn what they're up to. After the other night, I've got no use for Shane Wren and the rest of his cronies."

"You should go," said Madison.

"Me too," chimed in Alex.

"I don't really think this will be appropriate for—" started Madison before Colton interrupted her.

"It'll be fine, Maddie, and instructive. Alex can see how these types of meetings are conducted. Also, another set of eyes and ears will help."

"Yeah," said Alex as she ran to find her shoes.

When she returned, she kissed her Mom on the cheek. "Thanks, Mom. I really want to help, but I also need to get out of the house. I'm getting cabin fever."

"Good grief." Madison laughed. "After one day. Are you guys leaving already?"

"Yeah," started Colton. "I wanna check on Mrs. Abercrombie, and then I might pick up the Youngs and Kaplans on the way to the meeting. I love you." Colton kissed Madison on the cheek. He and Alex were off on their father-daughter afternoon. The usual afternoon of golf together was replaced with checking on neighbors and neighborhood association meetings.

Colton and Alex spent about five minutes knocking on Mrs. Abercrombie's doors and walking around her home. She never answered. The doors were locked, and there were no signs of a break-in.

"This is weird, Daddy," said Alex. "Mom and I saw Mrs. Abercrombie getting her mail two days ago. Surely she didn't go anywhere, right?"

"I don't see her car, and everything else seems to be okay," replied Colton. "Maybe she got spooked by the news and went over to a friend's home for safety."

Alex shrugged and led the way to the Youngs' front door. Nobody was home, but their note, if they received one, was missing. As they walked back across their front yard towards the Kaplans, the smell of smoke became more intense as the hot winds picked up.

"Daddy, it hasn't rained in a week, at least," started Alex. "I remember because our match got rained out."

"It's a bad situation," said Colton. "I'm sure other transformers exploded Thursday night. Those fireballs could have gone throughout the city, catching houses and trees on fire. With no firefighting equipment available and no water being pumped, the fires will burn uncontrolled until it rains."

"Hey, Colton!" shouted Rusty Kaplan from his driveway. "Did you hear about the meeting?"

"Yeah," replied Colton. "Do you guys wanna go with us?"

"Sounds good," replied Karen Kaplan.

The four began walking up the hill towards the Brileys' home. One of their neighbors was the listing agent on the vacant house and apparently made it available to Wren for the meeting. They walked slowly as Karen and Rusty became winded on the fairly steep incline of Lynnwood Boulevard.

"What do you expect from this meeting?" asked Rusty, now out of breath.

"I guess it makes sense to establish a system of community leadership," started Colton. "Assuming this situation is going to go on for a while, our neighbors in need could benefit from somebody looking out for them."

"What do you think about Shane?" asked Karen.

"No comment." Colton laughed. The Kaplans had puzzled looks on their faces. Colton realized they didn't understand, and he cautioned himself against expressing his opinion like that in the future. Words were amplified now and could easily become misconstrued. "Well, Shane is a professor of political science. He should have an idea how groups and governments are formed. I'm hoping for the best."

They reached the top of the hill and the street leveled out. Several people were making their way towards the Briley residence.

"Almost there," Rusty huffed.

"Let me add this," said Colton. "In my opinion, the best way to form an impromptu group is to establish a committee of leaders, with one person being the primary spokesman. If everyone votes on their leadership team, this will help boost morale and give folks a sense of security. The team would also gain respect through legitimacy. Under the circumstances, a little structure may lend some normalcy to everyone who is used to functioning with a government in our lives."

"Do you think Shane is the right man for the job?" asked Karen.

"I only know him in passing, Karen," replied Colton. "I think any leader needs to have the respect of the entire community and should have a track record of moral integrity. He needs to set an example for the neighborhood and make sound decisions. Only time will tell if he is the right guy for the job."

CHAPTER 11

DAY TWO
Noon, September 10
HPA Meeting House
Trimble Rd. & Lynnwood Blvd.
Belle Meade, Tennessee

"Here we go," said Alex, who had remained quiet the entire way. She recognized this as an adult meeting and was glad to get out of the house. If she were able to help in some way, maybe her dad would bring her again. Colton leaned into her ear and whispered, "Watch, listen, and learn," as they entered the grand foyer of the large home, which had been on the market since the previous year. The Brileys were divorced, and the court ordered the sale of the home. It stood vacant, as the spiteful couple refused to live in it.

"Welcome, folks," said Shane Wren as he opened up the double set of sliding doors leading to a covered patio that stretched the length of the home. "Let's go out here. This is a big turnout, and it'll be much cooler in the shade of this canopy."

Alex looked around at the attendees. They were all dressed like a normal day. Nobody seemed panicked or injured. A couple of parents had brought their young children, who attempted to squirm out of their parents' control. All of the neighbors appeared overheated. As everyone found a spot, Alex noticed there was only one other teenager, who was standing alone at the back of the enclosed patio. She tugged on her dad's arm and whispered, "I'm gonna hang out with the kid on the back wall, okay?"

"Sure, but don't wander off," replied Colton.

"Got it," she replied.

Alex nonchalantly walked toward the back of the patio and leaned against the wall. The boy immediately noticed her, but shyly looked away when she caught his glance. He appeared to be a year or two younger than Alex. Alex turned her attention to Wren as he started the meeting.

"Thank you, everyone, for coming this afternoon. I see a lot of familiar faces, but for those who don't know me, my name is Shane Wren, and I live through the backyard behind us on Westview. My wife, Christie, is at home with our two young daughters. In my prior life, which was, well, a couple of days ago, I was a professor at Vandy." The group laughed with Wren. Alex didn't, and she noticed that her dad wasn't laughing either.

"I've been the president of the Harding Place Association, or the HPA as we like to call it, for almost two years. In the past, my job was to organize activities and deal with issues surrounding our restrictions. Today, we face an uncertain future and a crisis never before experienced in our country."

Several people mumbled their acknowledgement of the situation and nodded as Wren continued. A few attendees carried notepads and used them as fans to cool their faces.

"I would like to introduce a couple of your neighbors. This is Adam Holder, who used to work for First Tennessee Bank."

Holder stepped forward. "Hello, everyone."

"Adam lives down on the cul-de-sac at Sheppard Place," started Wren. "Also, please meet Gene Andrews, who lives right up the street. Gene has an announcement to make, don't you, Gene?"

"I do," said Andrews. "I was formerly director of compliance at the IRS office here in Nashville. I'm pleased to announce that we won't be collecting taxes for a while." The three men laughed and several in the crowd joined in.

"Our life is over and they want to spew a bunch of jokes," said the teenage boy into Alex's ear, startling her. She jumped and turned toward him.

"You scared me!" she exclaimed.

"Sorry, dude," said the boy. "I didn't mean to." He cut himself off and hung his head. Alex picked up on the fact that he was sensitive to being scolded.

"It's okay," she started. "I'm a little jumpy, you know. My name's Alex."

"Hi. My name is Jimmy." He hesitated for a moment. "Jimmy Holder. That's my stepdad up there—the one with the sport coat on."

"It's a little hot for a jacket, isn't it?" asked Alex as Wren continued.

"He's a banker, whadya expect?" Jimmy replied, drawing a laugh from Alex. Jimmy kicked a small rock and chuckled under his breath.

Wren spoke a little louder. "Make room for these new folks who've just arrived, if you don't mind." The outdoor room became more crowded as a few more joined the group. Alex estimated forty people were crammed into the small space.

Wren continued. "Until the government gets things squared away, we've decided to meet here every day at noon. Of course, attendance isn't mandatory, but we hope all of you will play an active role in binding our community together. We have every confidence that FEMA will be reaching out to all of our neighborhoods."

Spontaneous applause erupted from much of the room. Alex smirked and shook her head. *They don't know that for certain.*

Jimmy must have noticed her reaction and quietly spoke to Alex. "They're blowing sunshine," he started. "My stepdad says the power may not come on for years. He's worried about the fact we don't have much food."

"You don't?" asked Alex.

"He'd usually eat out after work, while at the bar," said Jimmy. "He'd make me fend for myself when Mom was traveling."

"Where is she?" asked Alex.

"D.C.," he replied. "She's a bank lobbyist."

"Oh," said Alex. She studied Jimmy. He seemed troubled and distant. Alex had met kids like him in the past. Broken homes often didn't work out for the children. Parents couldn't get along, split up, and then remarried. Some kids took it in stride—many couldn't cope.

Jimmy seemed to fall into the latter category.

Wren continued speaking. "Our President wants us to band together, pool our resources, and help one another through this crisis. In the spirit of cooperation, we are asking our neighbors—all of you and those who couldn't attend today—to bring extra food, water, and supplies to our daily meetings."

Alex asked, "Does he drink *a lot?*"

Jimmy nodded his head as he looked down. "I don't think my stepdad ever wanted to be a father. He liked my mom, and they got married. I was part of the package deal. His priorities are my mom, a full liquor cabinet, and his big gun collection. I don't even think I rate in the top ten on the list."

Wren was winding up the meeting. "Also, please check on your immediate neighbors. Make sure they're safe. If they're not home, make a note of their address and bring it with you to the next meeting. We'll pay particular attention to their homes while they're away."

Alex looked up from the rock Jimmy was rolling around under his black Converse sneaker. She studied his clothes. Black, frayed shorts. An AC/DC tee shirt. Black hair and an earring. His appearance screamed rebellious teen.

Alex, like her father, was a Type A personality. If she weren't a girl, she'd be an alpha male. She sensed weakness in Jimmy. His mentioning a big gun collection presented an opportunity for the Rymans. Apparently, Jimmy didn't know the *loose lips sink ships* rule.

Chapter 12

DAY THREE
10:00 a.m., September 11
Ryman Residence
Belle Meade, Tennessee

"Mom, there are wildfires burning out of control all over the country," said Alex as her mother walked into the living room. The Rymans were settling into their routine by the start of day three.

Like most families, their previous life was full of activities—work, school, and household chores. Entertainment in the form of television, music, and computer browsing would take up hours of a typical day. Without power, these regular pursuits no longer existed. Security was most important followed by information gathering.

"How'd you find that out?" asked Madison.

Alex wound the crank handle of the ETON FRX3 radio made to the specifications of the American Red Cross. The rechargeable weather alert radio with a solar panel and hand turbine power generator not only provided information, but it had a USB auxiliary input to charge other devices.

"The emergency alerts are being broadcast continuously now. The message from yesterday is still being repeated, but NOAA is also issuing warnings for specific areas of the country. The wildfires are everywhere because of the heat."

When the power grid collapsed, cell phone service and normal broadcast networks crashed with it. However, the military had its own parallel intranet and secured closed satellite communications systems. The National Oceanic and Atmospheric Administration, NOAA, and several other dedicated radio stations across the AM band operated within the same shielded wiring system as the military.

When the airwaves weren't cluttered with cell phone calls and radio station broadcasts, a signal could travel much farther. By retuning the frequency calibration of a radio, it was possible to pick up ham radio operators near the AM frequencies.

"Here, grab a bucket," said Madison. She and Alex walked outside to the pool, scooped up a five-gallon bucket of pool water and carried them into the bathrooms. Although the power outage prevented the toilets from refilling on their own, the tank lid could be removed and refilled manually, enabling the toilet to function.

"Can I go with Dad to the meeting again?" asked Alex.

"Sure," replied Madison. "Is it because of the boy you met?"

"No, not really," replied Alex. She had an idea but didn't want to mention it to her parents yet. They'd probably overreact and make her stay home. "I don't know. He's younger than me and not at all cute. *Different* is a better word. It's just nice to talk to someone else, do you know what I mean?"

They parted ways and refilled the tanks of the four bathroom home. Afterwards, they reconvened in the living room.

"I understand, dear," said Madison, stacking the buckets for later use. She wiped the sweat off her brow. "It gets pretty boring around here. But I suppose that's a good thing under the circumstances."

Colton entered the room, dripping in sweat. "Do you think a dip in the pool is out of the question?"

"Duh, Dad," replied Alex. "That's our drinking water."

"How about a shower?" asked Madison. "It'll be cool, but we can easily make it hot."

"All right, let's see," said Colton.

Madison led them to the back patio, where she had hung the five-gallon camp shower purchased the other day at the sporting goods store. Made of black PVC material, it was solar heated and portable. She had hung it from the roof overhang at the pool house.

Madison reached up and squeezed the bulb, allowing water to pour through a flexible hose. "Voila, now we can clean up here instead of the pool," she announced. "Here's a bucket to be used for soapy water, and you can always douse yourself with a five-gallon bucket for a final rinse."

"I love it," said Colton, who immediately stripped down to his shorts and poured water over his head. "I need to get cleaned up for the second showing of the HPA program featuring Wren and Company."

"I'm going with you, Daddy," said Alex.

"Great," started Colton.

"What's with all the sandbags?" asked Madison. Colton had retrieved them at dusk last night and spent the last hour moving them upstairs.

"Let me explain. I saw them the other day protecting the manhole opening near Mrs. Abercrombie's house." Colton quickly toweled himself off. He reached for the dry pair of shorts and slipped them on under his towel. "They may be very useful at some point."

Colton continued to wipe himself off as he led the girls inside. They followed him to the top of the stairs, where several sandbags were stacked along the banister. He continued. "When somebody kicks in our doors, you can be pretty sure the people coming in are not here to make friendly conversation or to borrow a cup of sugar. We need to be prepared to defend ourselves and to greet them with a sufficient amount of deterring force."

"Are we gonna drop the sandbags on their heads like in the *Home Alone* movie, Daddy?"

Colton laughed. "I hadn't thought of that, Alex, but it's a possibility. I've tried to think of as many scenarios as possible so that we can maximize our defenses against bad guys. If we get overrun, we need a rallying point and methods to delay our attackers while everybody gets together."

"You've placed sandbags near the dormer windows too," noticed Madison.

Colton patted a stack of sandbags. "These are solid and will help deflect or absorb any bullets shot at us. Whether we're shooting from the windows or keeping them from coming up the stairs, the goal is to delay, then defend against the intruders."

"Makes sense," said Alex. "What about the dressers?"

Colton easily pushed one of the dressers to block the stairs. He tilted the dresser and retrieved one of the felt EZ slides from beneath the furniture leg.

"I found these in the utility room," said Colton. "The movers used them to push the heavy pieces of furniture around the house. If our attackers are pursuing us up the stairs, blocking their way with a heavy piece of furniture should slow them down."

"Won't we get trapped up here?" asked Madison.

"I have a plan for that," replied Colton. "This is a fallback position if we can't get to the rally point through the downstairs exits."

"Where is the rally point?" asked Alex.

"The garage, where our most valuable asset is located." Colton led them past the bedroom toward the double-door entry to the bonus room—a six-hundred-square-foot space located above the garage—which was built into the roof truss system. The family once used it to shoot pool and play video games.

More sandbags were stacked in front of the pool table. Under the pool table was an area rug. Colton dropped onto his hands and knees, pulled aside the rug, and revealed a two-foot-by-three-foot opening in the floor between the trusses.

Madison and Alex crawled under the pool table to look as well. "A hidey hole," exclaimed Alex. The three of them looked into the garage, where the roof of the Jeep Wagoneer was parked a few feet below them.

"We're gonna practice this until it becomes easy," said Colton. "But the plan would be to lure them up the stairs, delay their access to the second floor, and then drop ourselves through this hole and into the Wagoneer."

"You mean we'll leave everything behind?" asked Madison.

"Not entirely," replied Colton. "We need to pack the truck with clothing, supplies, and food. Use every available suitcase, duffle bag, and backpack."

"I should also put the camping supplies and fishing gear in the back," added Madison. "We don't need them here."

Colton slid out from underneath the pool table and bumped his head in the process. "Defending our home against armed gunmen is our biggest weakness. We only have one weapon, and none of us are trained. A gunfight is not conducive to on-the-job training. All of these measures are designed to delay the attack so we can escape."

"Live to fight another day," added Alex.

"Exactly."

CHAPTER 13

DAY THREE
Noon, September 11
HPA Meeting House
Trimble Rd. & Lynnwood Blvd.
Belle Meade, Tennessee

The second meeting of the HPA took place in front of the house in the circle drive. Attendance was larger today. Alex saw the Youngs and the Kaplans hanging out under a large oak tree. They'd had a conversation about this on the way over to the meeting.

Colton felt like they were better off than most of their neighbors thanks to the efforts of Madison and Alex. The acquisition of the Jeep Wagoneer in a world full of the latest and greatest, but now inoperable, vehicle transportation was very fortunate.

In the past seventy-hours, they'd not heard any generators running. This could be because no one in the vicinity owned one or because they didn't have the fuel to run it. Either way, the Rymans had both and would shield these assets from others as well.

With this in mind, the Rymans decided to blend in and not stick out. The plan was to dress normal and move and act in a way that was forgettable. They agreed to use their best efforts not to draw unnecessary attention to themselves. If their neighbors realized the extent of their supplies, they would become jealous or even angry. As time passed, that anger could turn to desperation and violence.

"Invisible in plain sight," Alex whispered to her dad as they walked to the middle of the pack.

Wren walked onto the front porch of the home, followed by his two sidekicks—Holder and Andrews. The grand appearance of the anointed leaders of the HPA disgusted Alex. She could see disdain on a few of her neighbors' faces as well. She quickly glanced through the crowd, looking for Jimmy Holder. She couldn't see him.

Then, a moment later, three men in mismatched uniforms joined them. They were carrying sidearms and had rifles slung over their shoulders. They looked like they were military or National Guardsmen.

"May I have your attention, please," started Wren. "Once again, I want to thank all of you for attending. I anticipated a bigger turnout today, so I moved the meeting to the front yard. I apologize for the heat, but the shade trees and the slight breeze should make it more comfortable."

Wren turned and received a clipboard from Holder, with a pen tied to it by a string. Wren continued. "I'd like everyone present today to sign in with your name and address, if you don't mind. In order to help one another, we need to know who is here. Also, if you have any special requirements like medications, please note them on the notepad or see Gene, Adam, or myself after the meeting. We will begin to pool our limited resources and distribute them to those who are in need."

Wren walked to the front of the crowd and began to pass the clipboard around. As it circulated, one of the uniformed men leaned into Wren and whispered in his ear. Colton shifted uneasily as he fixed his eyes on the three men. Alex picked up on his reaction to their attendance.

"Dad, what's wrong?"

"I don't like the looks of these guys," he replied.

Alex studied them further. Their uniforms didn't match, but there might be an explanation for that under the circumstances. Then she looked at their shoes. They weren't military-style leather boots. The men were wearing hunting boots like you buy at Walmart.

Alex leaned into her father and whispered, "Daddy, their shoes."

Colton nodded. "It wouldn't surprise me if they're imposters," said Colton. "Look at how they stand. Their demeanor is off somehow. There's no *discipline*."

Wren began the meeting. "I'm pleased to let all of you know that our government is hard at work to fix this situation, and they have placed the National Guard on the streets of Nashville to ensure we are protected—which leads me to the introduction of these three gentlemen."

Wren explained the men were part of the National Guard contingent assigned to their area. They would be checking on missing neighbors and helping the sick get to hospitals. As he spoke, the clipboard made its way to Colton, and he immediately passed it on to a person behind him.

"Aren't you gonna sign it?" asked Alex.

"Nope, none of their business," he replied under his breath.

Wren continued. "These men will spearhead the recovery effort in the Belle Meade area and keep us informed of newsworthy events and further emergency alerts."

As Wren spoke, Alex saw Jimmy Holder emerge from around the large shrubs at the corner of the HPA meeting house. He seemed disinterested in Wren's presentation, opting instead to break off a piece of a boxwood and pick off its leaves.

Alex took a deep breath and whispered to her dad, "Daddy, do you trust me?"

"Of course, Allie-Cat."

"Okay," she continued, leaning closer so she wouldn't be overheard. "I'm gonna leave now, and I'll meet you back at the house. I'll be safe, I promise."

"But wait," Colton replied, but Alex was off, casually working her way through the crowd while their attention was focused on the front porch. In less than a minute, she reached Jimmy's side.

"Hey, you," she started, getting Jimmy's attention. He managed a sheepish smile before returning to the task of de-leafing the boxwood branch.

"Hey."

"Pretty boring, huh?" asked Alex.

"Yeah. I don't have to be here, but what else is there to do?"

Alex thought for a moment. She was sure this boy was harmless.

The plan she was about to embark upon could prove dangerous if he turned out to be a teen wolf in black sheep's clothing.

She gathered up her courage and spoke. "You wanna go somewhere? I mean, this is such a waste, right?"

"For sure," replied Jimmy. His attitude picked up. "Where do you wanna go?"

"Not my house," she replied. "My mom's there, and it would be, well, you know, *awkward*."

"We could go over to my place, I guess," said Jimmy. "We don't have any video games or TV though. We could just hang out."

"That sounds good to me," said Alex. "Lead the way."

Jimmy ducked around the corner of the house, and Alex took one more glance for her dad, but she couldn't see him. There was no turning back now. Alex darted after Jimmy through the backyards, the rush of adrenaline providing an exhilaration she'd never felt before.

She was an *undercover operative*!

CHAPTER 14

DAY THREE
12:15 p.m., September 11
Holder Residence
Belle Meade, Tennessee

Alex followed Jimmy through the open garage and directly inside. The garage was full of plastic storage bins. She tried her best to inventory the contents, but she didn't want Jimmy to catch her snooping. The big prize was inside.

"Sorry for the mess," started Jimmy as he led her into the house. "My mom is the only one who cleans up around here, and she sucks at it. Our house is so messy they won't even hire a cleaning service to come in. Look around. What's the point?"

"It's not that bad," Alex lied. The place was a pigsty. Empty pizza boxes and beer cans were strewn about. His stepdad, a smoker, must not have been interested in emptying his ashtrays. The stale air coupled with the stench of beer and cigarettes almost caused Alex to retch, but she contained herself.

Jimmy showed Alex his room and revealed his *Walking Dead* comic book collection. He had a duplicate of issue 100 in which Negan killed Glenn, so he gave it to Alex as a gift. She thought that it was sweet and thanked him. She did plan to read it later. *First things first.*

She engaged in some small talk with Jimmy but was very much aware of the time. After the HPA meeting broke up, his stepdad might come home. Her new friendship with Jimmy needed to be kept under wraps.

Alex saw a slightly open door under the stairwell. It appeared to be the stairs that led into the basement. She nonchalantly bumped into the doorknob as she walked past, causing it to open further.

"Ouch," she exclaimed, pretending to get bruised by the collision. As the door swung open, she asked, "What's down there?"

"Oh, yeah," started Jimmy as he reached down and picked up a battery-operated Coleman lantern. "You wanna see my stepdad's gun vault?"

"I guess," she tried to appear aloof. "I've never seen a gun before."

"Never?"

"Nope," she replied, twisting a strand of her long blonde hair. "Do you mind showing me?"

Jimmy shrugged and turned on the light. The two reached the bottom of the stairs, which opened to a large unfinished basement. Once downstairs, he turned on three other Coleman lanterns, revealing a series of workbenches and pegboards. There were several gun safes, but two of them were open. Several dozen green military-issue ammo cans were stacked neatly under the benches.

Alex was genuinely amazed. "Wow," she uttered. "He's ready for a war."

"I guess," said Jimmy. "He's always going to gun shows. He buys and sells, then brags about the great deals he made. I've been with him when he buys guns from online sellers."

Alex walked through the room and nonchalantly picked up some of the weapons. *This was a gold mine!*

"I didn't know you could buy guns on the Internet," said Alex, appearing to be interested while she took a mental inventory. She didn't know what these guns were called, but she knew how to count. There were two dozen pistols, more than a dozen rifles, and several that looked like machine guns.

"He went on these two websites several times a day looking for new listings," said Jimmy. "One is called Armslist and the other is called Tennessee Gun Owners. He was obsessed with buying and selling. But as you can see, he mostly bought."

"Do you know how to shoot?" asked Alex.

"Of course."

"Would you teach me?" Alex was going to appear weak and vulnerable in order to appeal to Jimmy's *man-as-protector* side if he was old enough to have one. "Because, well, I'm kinda afraid of everything. Do you know what I mean?"

"Sure," he replied.

Alex glanced back at him and noticed that he was studying her long legs. He was just fourteen years old, but he was still a boy. She'd have to keep an eye on him. For the moment, he aimed to please, and she intended to take advantage.

That was when she saw it. A real Taurus PT111 like the replica her mother had purchased at Phillips Toy Mart. It was stuck in a holster that would slide into the waistband of her jean shorts. She debated whether to take it or ask Jimmy for it. She decided to ask.

Alex picked up the gun and held it in her hands. She walked toward Jimmy and got close enough to him so he would feel slightly uncomfortable.

"This one," she said. "I think this one would be perfect for me, don't you agree, Jimmy?"

"Yeah, sure," he replied nervously. "That's a great choice. You can have it. My stepdad won't, um, know. Here's a box of ammo too."

Jimmy handed her a box of nine-millimeter ammunition. She took the box, and the weight pulled her arm down.

"Whoa." She laughed. "That's heavy."

"There's fifty rounds in each box. We can start training tomorrow."

Suddenly, their attention was drawn to the stairs. A noise was coming from outside the house. A voice. Alex immediately became nervous and looked around. With Jimmy preoccupied, she slid the paddle holster into her waistband and snatched another box of ammo off the bench.

Jimmy sprinted up the stairs and she followed him. She ran after him, almost tripping over an empty liquor bottle on the floor. As he opened the front door, the sound became clear.

Down the street, a green military Humvee was driving slowly. A soldier stood outside the turret, resting his arms on a fifty-caliber machine gun. The passenger repeated the message.

"This is an alert. All residents are advised to shelter in place. I repeat. Stay in your homes. The National Weather Service has advised us of another solar storm, which will take place in the next twelve hours. This storm will contain a high radiation index. You are advised to remain in your homes for the next twelve hours."

Alex watched the Humvee disappear down the street as the message was read again. She tucked the two boxes of ammo against her left side and held the gun against her right. She leaned down and gave Jimmy a kiss on the cheek.

"Thank you, Jimmy," she said. "This was fun. Can I come over tomorrow at noon?"

A smitten Jimmy Holder touched his cheek and nodded—having no idea he'd just been played.

CHAPTER 15

DAY FOUR
Morning, September 12
Ryman Residence
Nashville, Tennessee

Madison and Colton had become like two ships passing in the night. By the fourth day, their sleeping routines were established. Colton's body gradually adjusted to staying awake until dawn, and Madison reset her internal clock to wake up early enough to fix them something to eat. Breakfast gave them some quiet time together before she took over the security patrols while Colton slept. It was time for the morning debrief, and the first item on the agenda was Alex's new friend.

"Maddie, I understand your concern," started Colton. "While I stood watch last night, I considered all of the ramifications of Alex's actions. First, I'm glad we've got a great relationship with her so she wouldn't hide what she did. Second, I trust her judgment. It was a risky, apparently unplanned move."

"Impulsive is more like it," interrupted Madison, who sat back in the dining chair and folded her arms. Madison's body language delivered her opinion of Alex's acquisition of the gun loud and clear.

"Maybe, but I like *quick-thinking* better. Even when the kids heard the military vehicle driving through the neighborhood and the boy bolted outside ahead of her, Alex had the presence of mind to grab another box of bullets. You can't teach that cleverness in school, Maddie. It's ingrained in her DNA."

"Oh, of course, she's a full-blooded Ryman without a doubt," said Madison.

"Don't forget, *Mrs. Ryman*," Colton said sarcastically. "As part of her ruse, she used her power of feminine persuasion over the boy. I seem to remember a young woman who exerted a similar influence over the master negotiator in this family many years ago."

"Okay." Madison laughed and wiped a couple of tears off her face. Colton reached across the table and held her hand. In the candlelight of the early dawn of the apocalypse, she was more beautiful than ever.

"Here's the other thing," said Colton. "Over the years, I've learned that before I enter any negotiation session, I like to clarify my goals and gather information about the other side before I sit at the table. Alex gleaned some important information yesterday. We have a neighbor who's armed to the hilt."

"And he's got a screw loose," interjected Madison. "What if he finds out about this?"

"It's risky, but our goal shouldn't be to clean out his basement, only to get what we really need. Remember, his son offered the gun and ammo to Alex as a gift. I'm only suggesting that she ask for one or two more weapons for her parents."

"Fair enough," said Madison. "But if we only need a couple more guns, why don't we just trade him some food. Jimmy told Alex they don't have any food, right?"

"I thought about that, but here's my concern. If Holder thinks we have extra, expendable food, with his arsenal, he might just take it from us. It's better to keep him out of the loop and keep our food storage to ourselves."

"So what's the plan?" asked Madison.

"I'll talk with her on the way to the meeting today," replied Colton. "Two more guns. Another handgun similar to the one she obtained yesterday and one of those machine-gun-type rifles she told us about. Common sense tells me the high-capacity magazines would help repel anyone trying to attack us in our home."

Madison relented. "Alex is very levelheaded and won't take a chance if the risk is too great. She plans on going over there at noon today. Maybe you can stall Holder if the meeting breaks up early?

You know, give her more time."

Colton scooped up the paper plates and forks from breakfast and placed them into the garbage bag. Monday was usually garbage pickup day, except not anymore. He needed to talk to Madison about scavenging. Colton was aware the topic would concern Madison because it involved taking Alex with him, after dark, into the homes of strangers.

With each passing day, Madison seemed to accept the reality of this catastrophic event. Her lingering denial was passing, and fear seemed to be on her mind the most. Without putting her on edge, Colton had to find the words to explain why he was using her only child as an undercover operative by day and now a cat burglar by night. Both activities had inherent risks, but in a post-apocalyptic world, children learned to grow up fast.

"Can we talk about one more thing before I get some sleep?" he asked.

"Yes, but you need to get your rest. The *evil sun* is rising for another day, just like always."

Colton sat back down and fiddled nervously with the salt and pepper mills on the kitchen table. He was convinced this collapsed-grid situation was going to be prolonged and have a severe impact on the entire country for weeks or months. While he was relieved to have the additional food and supplies stacked around their dining room, he knew it wouldn't be enough to last them.

"You guys did great the other day, Maddie," started Colton. "You risked your lives for our family—our survival."

"Aw shucks, 'tweren't nuthin'." Madison chuckled as she subconsciously touched her cheek, which was finally returning to its normal color.

"It was a lot," said Colton. "But it may not be enough. As our food and supplies dwindle, or if something happens, God forbid, and everything gets destroyed or stolen, we might run out. I think we need to get more."

"What are you suggesting?"

"I don't believe the government has enough food and supplies to go around. Even if they do, how will they be rationed and for how long? We have to look at alternative resources."

"Looting," said Madison.

"I prefer the term scavenging."

"Stealing," Madison shot back, once again assuming a defiant position. "Are we supposed to throw His Ten Commandments out with the garbage today?"

"Maddie, please hear me out," pleaded Colton. Before he broached the subject, Colton was most concerned about Madison's reaction to his use of Alex as a partner in crime. Now, the bigger obstacle appeared to be the moral issue.

Madison continued. "I understood taking the scrap lumber from the home under construction. Even the sandbags can be returned when this whole thing is over. The stuff from the O'Malleys', well, that's a little different."

Colton didn't want to argue, especially under these stressful circumstances. He didn't want to do things behind Madison's back either. He'd tell her how he felt, and they'd decide together.

"There's a big difference between scavenging and looting," started Colton. "Searching for food or salvaging supplies from abandoned homes is much different than taking something by force."

"Word games."

"Maybe, but my point is there can be extenuating circumstances that allow an exception to the rule of thou shalt not steal. Many of these homes are abandoned. It's just a matter of time before our neighbors or outsiders break into them. If we wait until we're almost out of food, there won't be any opportunities to scavenge left."

Madison stared at him for a moment. "What if the people come back? These are our neighbors we're talkin' about."

"Then we will gladly reimburse them somehow for the supplies we used," he replied. "Listen, we're in a survival situation. I'm not advocating loading up on mink coats, stereos, or valuable family heirlooms. In my opinion, anything that does not fulfill our basic human needs—water, food, shelter, security, and energy—stays behind. Otherwise, it would be looting."

"The law of necessity."

"That's a good way of looking at it," said Colton. "Taking the highest social morality may not always be achieved by adherence to the laws of God or man. There is no greater goal than the survival of our family. In doing so, if I technically violate those laws, including the Eighth Commandment, then I will be judged at some point. But my family will be alive."

CHAPTER 16

DAY FOUR
Dusk, September 12
Ryman Residence
Belle Meade, Tennessee

The noon meeting of the HPA had been canceled due to the second solar storm announced by the National Guardsmen the day before. Colton was able to get some extra sleep for the big night ahead. His goal was to make two stops. One would be the O'Malleys' home. The second on the list was a little further down the street next to the home under construction. He'd studied the surroundings of both homes during his prior outings.

"Alex, all I know is what I've seen on television and by applying common sense," explained Colton. He pulled the grocery totes out of the pantry and set them on the counter next to their backpacks. "These are going to fill up very quickly and get heavy even faster. If all goes well, we'll be able to make several trips without detection. After the second solar storm the northern lights will be bright again tonight, so we'll have to stay concealed. Fortunately, we don't have far to go."

"Okay, Daddy," said Alex. "Tell me what to focus on before we leave. Also, what if something happens and we split up? Do I wait on you or head back to the house?"

"Great question, Alex. If we're discovered and threatened, then drop everything. Run through the yards but not directly home. We don't need to draw them to our front door. Your mom will be patrolling the front yard, watching for signs of trouble. She'll help if possible."

Madison lifted the shotgun off the kitchen counter. The family had spent the day practicing. They emptied the shotgun and the pistol of ammunition. They practiced loading and reloading. Then they moved on to dry-fire drills.

Throughout the day, each of them took turns. With the paddle holster firmly in place, they repeatedly drew their pistols until the practice created muscle memory and conditioned their reflexes. If they had to challenge someone or draw to shoot, they could ready their weapon as if it was second nature. As Alex pointed out, it was no different than practicing her golf swing—grip, stance, tempo, and concentration.

They learned trigger control and aim. Using a small picture hanging on the wall as a target, they drew the weapon and pointed it at the target. As the shooter pulled the trigger, if the gun made a *click* with the sights still sitting on their point of aim, then that was considered a hit. If the sights moved off their target before the *click*, that would be a miss.

Using the toy versions of the Taurus, they practiced working through the house, looking for a hidden attacker. They emulated television shows they'd watched. Alex would hide while Madison and Colton hunted for her. They had to clear a room before they could move on to the next one. This exercise taught them how to work in pairs and watch each other's backs. It also enabled them to look at their home from a different perspective—as their fortress.

"I'll take the pistol," said Colton. "I want you to take this hunting knife your mom bought. We both have flashlights, but I want us to adjust our vision to the dark. The light will draw unnecessary attention to us."

"I'm ready," announced Alex. They both gave Madison a kiss and a hug.

As they made their way down the front yard, Madison took up a position under the cover of several oak trees adjacent to the Youngs' property. From there, she would have a clear view up and down both sides of the street. Colton chose the farthest location first. If their loads became too heavy, it would be better to travel the longer distance on fresh legs. He also wanted to glance at Mrs. Abercrombie's house to look for a burning candle or some sign of life. He was still troubled by her absence.

They reached the two-story tudor-style home owned by the Petersons. They were both in sales and frequently traveled. Most likely, they were stuck when the flights were grounded. Colton and Alex cautiously approached a hedgerow beside the house. Colton crouched down, and Alex knelt next to him.

"I want you to stay here for a moment," said Colton. "I'm going to walk around the house to make sure there hasn't been any forced entry. I don't want us going inside and meeting an unexpected occupant face-to-face."

Alex nodded and Colton was off. He worked his way around the unfamiliar home, being careful not to twist an ankle or cause unnecessary noise. Finding everything secure, he chose the rear French doors as the logical breach point.

He retrieved Alex and they approached the doors. Colton didn't want to draw attention by loudly breaking the glass, which was the easiest way to enter the house. He reached into his backpack for a roll of duct tape. He quickly taped one of the panes in the French door near the locks. He looked around for a large rock. The Petersons' yard was landscaped with medium-sized river rock, providing the perfect burglary tool. He gently cracked the pane and was pleased to see the majority of the glass remained stuck to the duct tape. After pulling the glass out of the way, Colton turned the bolt lock, unlocked the door handle, and they quickly stepped into the breakfast room undetected.

They were greeted with a rush of hot, stale air. That was a good sign to Colton. If the Petersons were home, windows allowing ventilation would've been opened. Nonetheless, he stuck to the plan and the initial item on the mental list.

"First, we clear the house just like we practiced," said Colton. They removed their backpacks and quietly walked through the downstairs and then made their way to the upper bedrooms. The house was empty and undisturbed. Colton breathed a sigh of relief and looked out the front and back windows. All appeared quiet.

"Should we start up here?" asked Alex.

Colton knew their priority was food, but another major item on the wish list was guns. If he could secure additional weapons, Alex could avoid another attempt to trick Jimmy Holder out of them.

"Okay, quickly," he replied. "The top priorities in the bedrooms are weapons, ammo, and medical supplies."

The two spent thirty minutes looking through closets and drawers, searching for any guns. There weren't any. They did find a couple of flashlights, and they emptied the master bath of a variety of medical supplies and toiletries. With Alex's backpack full, the two moved downstairs.

"What about this jewelry box, Dad?" asked Alex.

Colton thought about his discussion with Madison this morning, which had centered on the concept of scavenging versus looting. He considered taking the jewelry for its potential barter exchange value. He envisioned gold and silver becoming a new form of currency at some point. But how would Madison react? She would consider this stealing, pure and simple.

Alex provided the answer. "We could keep it safe for them until they come home."

"Safekeeping, good idea," said Colton. He took the jewelry box and headed down the stairs.

For the next hour, they gathered everything of post-apocalyptic value and organized it on the Petersons' breakfast table. From the utility room, they focused on bleach, cleaning supplies, and toilet paper.

The kitchen pantry was like so many American homes—relatively empty. The average household spent one hundred fifty dollars a week at the grocery store. Many Americans made one or two trips a week. Colton studied the paltry supply in the cupboards. Other than spices and some snacks, there was barely a week's worth of nonperishable food here.

"Load up my backpack and put the rest in the grocery totes," said Colton. "I wanna check the garage."

Colton found his way down the hallway into the pitch-black garage. The single window in the front of the house was covered with closed blinds. He turned on his small LED flashlight and pointed it low to the floor, which enabled him to find his way around. The Petersons had quite a few things of value, including a bag of cordless DeWalt power tools and battery chargers. There was also a half-full can of gasoline. Colton grabbed these two items and took a mental note of the remainder.

"Daddy, I'm ready," said Alex from the darkness of the kitchen. "There are dogs barking outside somewhere. I think we should go."

Colton picked up the pace and immediately chastised himself for lollygagging. He donned his backpack and slowly opened the back door. The dogs were barking loudly now. They appeared to be in the backyard of the home under construction.

WHAM! SHATTER!

The sound of breaking glass came from the home to their west, causing the dogs to be whipped into a hollerin' frenzy. Then he heard the voices.

"C'mon, man. Now listen to them dawgs."

"Sorry, bro! I didn't see the two-by-fours. Let's go. Ain't nothin' here no way."

"I'm gonna shut them dawgs up, man!"

The dogs were coming closer and becoming more agitated. Colton had to make a decision. Should they hide out here in the house until the looters left—which might risk a confrontation? Or should they leave everything behind and run for home?

The next thing that caught his eye helped him make a decision. The illumination of a flashlight was swinging wildly from the home behind the house next door.

"Who's out there? Go away!" shouted an elderly man.

"Shhhhh."

Colton heard the sound coming from between the houses. A shadow moved across the Petersons' back lawn. He felt for his weapon and almost drew it. Think! Options? The sounds of the dogs barking were much closer.

"Alex," instructed Colton, "they'll be distracted for a moment. Let's go out the front door. Run and take cover behind the cable repair truck. From there, we'll cross over into Mrs. Abercrombie's yard and make our way home under the tree canopy."

"Got it," said Alex, over the close sound of a snarling dog from the backyard.

"Get away from me, dawg!"

"Hey, let's go in this house," said one of the looters, heading right for Colton. Colton turned and dashed towards the front door and quietly closed it as he heard the voice again. "Hey, man, somebody beat us to it."

CHAPTER 17

DAY FIVE
11:00 a.m., September 13
Ryman Residence
Belle Meade, Tennessee

Colton opened the doors to the pool house and allowed the fumes from the generator to escape. This was the best of a lot of bad options to maintain some type of sound discipline. The world was very quiet now. There were no planes flying overhead. The thousands of cars traveling Harding Place each day were sidelined. The roar of air-conditioning units had ceased. Occasionally, a dog would bark in the distance or a voice would carry through the woods. But these ambient noises were insufficient to drown out the hum of his generator. By closing it up within the pool house, Colton trapped the noise, but the gas fumes reached deadly levels.

After a couple of minutes, he covered his face and immediately shut the generator off. He ran it for two hours a day to maintain the temperatures in the refrigerator and freezer and to allow Madison the opportunity to cook the day's meals. He also charged the flashlight batteries and the newly acquired DeWalt lithium ion batteries. He wasn't sure when he'd need the circular saw, drill, or reciprocating saw, but he was sure the portable shop light would come in handy.

"Daddy! There are people coming! Come quick!" shouted Alex from the French door.

Colton looked around frantically and closed the pool house door. He ran through the back door, feeling for his gun, but it wasn't there. He must've left it on the kitchen counter.

"Who is it?" asked Colton as he wiped his sweaty palms and sunscreen covered arms on his tee shirt. Madison came down the stairs and held her finger up to her lips. She mouthed the name *Shane Wren*.

Colton initially felt relieved. At least it wasn't the National Guard or a band of marauders—as Alex called the thugs and looters who roamed the streets. Then, on the other hand, a contingent of do-gooders operating under the pretense of being anointed the neighborhood watch was just as frightening. Colton recalled the quote from President Ronald Reagan: "The most terrifying words in the English language are *I'm from the government and I'm here to help*."

He decided nothing good was going to come out of this visit and immediately put his guard up. He walked toward the kitchen door. He would surprise them from the side of the house and throw them off their game from the beginning.

"Do you want the gun?" whispered Madison.

"No, I don't think that'll be necessary," replied Colton. "I'm gonna keep this to a friendly, neighborly chat."

"There are seven people out there," said Madison. "At least one man has a rifle over his shoulder, and another man has a gun tucked in the front of his jeans. They're here for a purpose."

"I'm sure they are. Maddie, go upstairs and monitor things from the window but try not to be seen. Alex, wait by the front door and be prepared to open it. Everybody good?"

Colton held the door handle as the girls ran to get in their positions. He took a deep breath and drew upon the confidence that had elevated him to the top of his field. He grabbed a screwdriver for a prop and exited into the sun. His exposed skin was drenched in sunscreen after the radiation warnings the other day.

Wren was approaching the front door as Colton walked around the corner of the house. Colton counted four men and three women. Wren was joined by Andrews, who was armed with a pistol, and Holder, who carried what Colton recognized as an AR-15. Even one of the women was armed. This was the new normal, he surmised.

"I guess you folks are here to fix our air-conditioning unit," said

Colton, attempting to break the ice. "You're a little late, but I'm glad you're here."

The group of seven turned and glared at him. No ice was broken.

"Ryman," started Wren, who stepped off the front porch and approached Colton, "this is not a social call. May we come in? We need to have a conversation."

Colton wasn't going to let peer pressure compromise their safety. "Nah," he drawled. "I think we can talk right here."

"Where's Madison?" asked one woman.

"And Alex?" chimed in one of the other women.

"They're inside," replied Colton. He turned his attention back to Wren. He was having difficulty being polite to people who were obviously loaded for bear. "How can I help you?"

"We think we need to get a few things straight," started Wren before the first woman spoke up again.

"We need to see Madison. We understand there was some *trouble* the other day and she might be injured."

Now Colton was pissed, but he didn't want to lose his composure. Madison had relayed the details of the unannounced visit by the Wrens the other night, so Colton understood where they were going with this conversation. He was going to shut this *witch hunt* down before it got out of hand.

"Madison told me that the Wrens stopped by the other night after she had been assaulted at the ATM. Let me repeat this for you all. Madison was assaulted on Thursday by a thug who tried to steal her money at the ATM. Alex had to save her. Nothing more, nothing less. Besides, none of this is any of your business, so you can take your phony concern and leave."

"Well, we just thought we should see if she needed anything," said the second woman, somewhat sheepishly compared to before.

Colton wasn't going to let them off the hook. "If you had genuine concern for my wife, you would've come by here on Friday morning. This is Tuesday and now you're concerned? I don't think so."

Colton paused and stared at Wren. He caught movement in the upper window above the front door. He was sure Madison was boiling mad. He hoped she didn't open fire on the group.

"Anything else?" he asked, staring at Wren.

"Well, Ryman, you just don't get it. We're trying to look after our neighbors and band together as a community. Everyone else seems to be on board with that, but not you."

"What's your point?" asked Colton.

"The point is our President has encouraged us to help one another through this crisis until FEMA and the National Guard can provide for everyone. Virtually the entire neighborhood seems to be with the program but you."

Colton didn't hesitate and shot back a response. "We don't have anything to contribute. I have to provide for the safety and welfare of my family first."

"Well, now, we think you do have lots to contribute, Ryman," said Holder brusquely. Colton immediately feared they knew about the Wagoneer, but it turned out their intentions were set on his next most valuable tool—the generator. "We could use that generator of yours for the benefit of the community."

"And the propane," added Andrews.

Colton hesitated for a moment. They could take it by force. *Deny.*

"I don't know what you're talking about. I think we're done here." Colton put his hands on his hips and studied their faces. *They know.*

Wren was incredulous, *probably because he was used to getting his way*, thought Colton. "I saw it, Ryman. Don't lie to us. I saw it in your Suburban the night Christie and I came over. The propane tanks too."

Well, crap. Last option—feigned outrage.

"Are you kidding me?" he shouted. "You show up at my home unannounced. You accuse me of beating my wife. And now I learn you've been snooping around my property and peering inside my vehicle? Hey, anything else I can do for you people?"

Wren tried to interrupt by raising both hands. "Listen, Ryman, the President has urged us to—"

"I don't give a crap! I'm *urging you* to get off my property. I'm done! You hear me? Go!"

Clack! Clack!

As if it was scripted, the distinctive sound of a shotgun racking a round came from the upper window. Everyone's attention was drawn upward, and Madison simply said, "You heard the man. We're done here."

Holder struggled to pull his AR-15 off his shoulder. Madison quickly pointed her shotgun directly at him.

"Easy now!" she shouted from the window, causing Holder to freeze immediately and spread his arms away from his body.

Wren looked at Colton and then turned back to his entourage. He nodded and mumbled, "Let's go." The group backed away slowly, and Colton took a couple of steps toward them to ensure their compliance.

"This isn't over, Ryman," hissed Wren

Colton stared him down and never broke eye contact. He suspected Wren was right.

The confrontation forced the Rymans into a decision they hadn't discussed in depth. They had the option of becoming actively involved with the HPA. Colton knew organizing the community with like-minded people was a good thing, and it would save lives. But he didn't share the same values and outlook as Wren and his friends.

Granted, the Ryman family wasn't as prepared as they could've been before this catastrophic event, but they were better off than most. Colton's job was to safeguard his family's safety and well-being. The day the solar storm was coming, Alex and Madison weren't fooling around, riding bicycles on the sidewalk like Christie Wren and her kids. They had hustled to prepare.

Why should he risk running out of food or give up vital supplies to those who didn't try to help themselves?

CHAPTER 18

DAY FIVE
6:00 p.m., September 13
Young Residence
Belle Meade, Tennessee

Madison hesitated to leave Alex at home alone, but Colton assured her they wouldn't be long. He wanted to touch base with the Youngs regarding the confrontation on the front lawn that morning and check on Mrs. Abercrombie once again.

It had been nearly two weeks since it had rained, and temperatures felt like they were in the nineties, if not a hundred plus. The unusual heat wave continued even after the sun had dealt its crushing blow, which exacerbated the water shortage and the potential for dehydration. After one to two days, weakness overtook the body. As people became dehydrated, they became irritable and confused. They would experience headaches, and their eyes would begin to appear sunken.

"Wren and the rest of that bunch at the HPA realize the weak will not survive," said Colton as they walked through the trees. "With each day, the other residents will coalesce around his leadership. Wren, Andrews, and Holder will convince our neighbors that binding together and staying in a group provides them strength in numbers."

"We don't have any numbers," added Madison.

"I know, which is part of the reason for this social call," said Colton.

As they stepped onto the Youngs' brick doorstep, the door opened and Diane Young appeared.

"Hey, neighbors," she greeted them. "I was just coming out to check the mail." The three laughed.

"We are creatures of habit," said Colton.

"More than you realize, if you'll indulge me for a moment," said Diane. "We are creatures and we have needs. We need to eat, so we eat. As intelligent and social animals, we like to chat with one another, so we do. We have dozens and dozens of other behaviors that are just as complicated."

"You and Bill would know," said Madison, referring to their profession as psychologists.

"Habits are one of those behaviors," said Diane. Her husband emerged from the foyer, wearing his customary khaki pants and blue button-down shirt. They were hanging on him. Madison wondered how much weight he'd lost. She continued. "Customs and practices help us make it through the day. This disaster has upset our normal lives, but our habits are still a part of our psyche."

"Which is why you're on your way to check the mail?" asked Madison, trying to psychoanalyze the psychologist.

"No." She laughed. "I was coming out here because I saw you coming through the trees. My goal is to provide you a reason to be careful. Every human deals with change differently. When a calamity strikes, turning one's habits, routines and life inside out, people react differently. Some become afraid. Others become angry at the rude intrusion upon their otherwise orderly lives. Those who are both fearful and angry will become dangerous due to their unpredictability."

"The human reaction we're describing was on full display today on your front lawn," added Bill. "Diane and I watched the confrontation from under the oaks. Colton, I don't wish to frighten you, but my observations of Wren and the HPA raise genuine concern for the safety of anyone who might oppose them."

"Physical harm?" asked Madison.

"Maybe," replied Bill. "Following a tragedy, and after reality sets in, an individual may exhibit anger at their condition. A person undergoing this phase might say—*why me* or *it's not fair!*"

"Others will be looking for someone to blame," added Diane. "When a logical target for their fear-induced anger is unavailable, they will seek out others. They'll lash out in frustration at those around them."

Madison became very nervous. She'd just pointed a gun at a group of neighbors who were exhibiting signs of a major depressive disorder. She unconsciously looked around her to see if anyone was coming.

"Well, I don't intend to have anything else to do with Wren or his band of do-gooders at the HPA," said Colton.

"Actually, that's the exact opposite of what you should do," said Bill. "You can't prevent others from talking behind your back. But by avoiding the group dynamic of the HPA, you're exhibiting guilt and weakness. Face your accusers and find a way to contribute without compromising your family's safety and well-being."

"I'll be outnumbered."

"We're your friends, Colton," said Diane. "We'll go with you if for no other reason than to be a character reference. Along with the Kaplans, we know you two better than anyone. I'm sure they would join us."

"They're right, Colton," said Madison. "I should go too. It will remind them we're a loving couple. Plus, I want to shut those nosy neighbor hens up once and for all."

Colton reached forward to shake Bill's hand, which turned into a hug. All of them embraced, which caused Madison to erupt with emotion.

"Thank you both so much," she sobbed. "This has been a difficult time for all of us. My daughter has seen things that I hoped she'd never be exposed to. Now, the whole neighborhood is rallying against us. It's hard to take, you know?"

Diane hugged Madison again and whispered to her, "You're not alone, dear. We'll help you as long as we can."

An approaching vehicle caught their attention. At first, it appeared to be a military truck, but upon closer inspection, Madison realized it was a GMC pickup painted in several shades of green, brown, and black to produce a camouflage effect.

"Those are the guys from the HPA meeting," said Colton.

"Indeed," added Bill. "They were supposedly National Guardsmen. Diane and I didn't buy it."

The truck slowed as the driver turned his attention to the O'Malley residence and then sped to the east. The back of the pickup was overfilled with clothing, tools, and some furniture pieces.

"They looked like they were moving rather than patrolling the neighborhood, looking for bad guys," said Madison. It was nearing dusk, and she wanted to check on Mrs. Abercrombie. She also had an odd feeling about those men. She wanted to get home to Alex. "Maybe we should get going, honey."

Once again the four neighbors exchanged hugs. The Youngs closed their door accompanied by the sounds of a bolt lock being engaged and a heavy piece of furniture being slid into place to block the door. Diane's words replayed in Madison's mind—*We'll help you as long as we can. What did she mean by that?*

CHAPTER 19

DAY FIVE
6:45 p.m., September 13
Abercrombie Residence
Belle Meade, Tennessee

Colton took a chair from Mrs. Abercrombie's patio set and placed it under the utility room window. He unclipped the small LED flashlight that accompanied him everywhere now, as did the Taurus tucked safely in the paddle holster. After today's confrontation, Colton vowed to remain armed at all times.

He flashed the light through the room, revealing a basket of neatly folded laundry and several bottles of bleach and detergent. With his last pass of the light along the floor, he caught a glimpse of something in the hallway. He shielded his eyes from the setting sun and focused them on the object. It was Mrs. Abercrombie's leg. She was sprawled out on the floor.

Colton, dejected and frustrated, knocked his head against the glass window several times. *I should have known.*

"Colton, what's wrong?" asked Madison, who had just returned from checking on Alex.

"We have to go inside. I've got a bad feeling about her." Colton lost his balance getting off the chair and landed in the grass on all fours.

"You okay?" asked Madison.

"Yeah," said Colton, wiping the grass off his still-battered knees. "Madison, um, I think she's dead."

Madison immediately covered her mouth and began to cry. Colton held her while she let out her emotions for the third time that day.

"Maddie, let me take you home. I'll come back and take care of this. I think you've had enough for one day."

Madison cried for a moment longer and then slowly gathered herself. She wiped away her tears. "No, I'm fine," she said. "I've got to hitch 'em up. It's just hard, you know?"

"I do, darlin'," said Colton. "Are you sure? I'm gonna have to bury her."

"We'll do it together," replied Madison.

Colton gently cracked the single pane of glass at the rear entrance to the garage. He reached for the doorknob to enter the home, but turned to Madison one last time and shined the light near her face. There was a dead body on the other side of this door. She reassured him with a forced smile and a nod.

Colton opened the door, and the smell of death immediately filled his nostrils. Colton quickly pulled his tee shirt over his mouth and nose. He turned around and stopped Madison from entering the hallway.

After death, the rate of decay within the human body was generally split into two distinct processes. Initially, rigor mortis, or the stiffening of the body, set in about two to six hours after death. Rigor was part of the first stage of self-digestion, where the body's enzymes went into a post-death meltdown. The process could be sped up by extreme heat and, likewise, slowed down by the cold.

The next stage was known as putrefaction, or decomposition, in which the body literally began the process of melting down. Bacteria and enzymes within the body broke down their host. The body became discolored—first turning green, then purple, and finally black. As the bacteria attacked the body, it created a putrid-smelling gas, which caused the body to bloat, the eyes to bulge out of their sockets, and the tongue to swell and protrude. Eventually, by day five, this gas had created enough internal pressure to release from the body's orifices.

"Madison, you should go home."

"My gosh, Colton. I had no idea."

"I've got to get in there and open some windows." Colton flashed his light toward an open Rubbermaid storage cabinet in the corner. It had a variety of yard-working tools, including goggles, gardening gloves, and allergy masks. *Perfect.*

Colton outfitted Madison and then himself. "Madison, listen to me," he instructed. "Do not look at her body. Do you understand me?"

"Yes," she mumbled through her mask. Madison adjusted her goggles. "Let's get it over with, please."

They entered the home as the ambient daylight disappeared. Within five minutes, all of the ground-floor windows were raised and the patio doors were propped open as well. Colton rummaged through a utility closet in the laundry room and found a set of sheets. He quickly covered Mrs. Abercrombie, who appeared to be clutching her chest when she died.

For people with a heart ailment, tomorrow was not a given. For those who lived with a pacemaker, the EMP blast from the solar flare resulted in certain death. These small, electronically sophisticated devices were placed in the chest to help control abnormal heart rhythms. They emitted low-energy electrical pulses to prompt the heart to beat at a normal rate. They were not made to withstand the incredible surge of energy created by an electromagnetic pulse.

The destruction of the pacemaker itself did not kill Mrs. Abercrombie. The combination of her slowed heart rate and the extreme heat wave they were experiencing probably made her weak, tired, and faint. She most likely lost consciousness and suffered a heart attack.

"Madison, would you mind finding a shovel? Then meet me in the backyard. Let's give her a proper burial."

An hour later, Colton and Madison were soaked in sweat, but Mrs. Abercrombie was provided a caring burial and eulogy by the Rymans. They both sat quietly for a moment before Madison broke the silence.

"Now what?"

Colton spotted a garden watering can placed under the drainpipe of the air-conditioning unit and decided to see if it contained water. It was half full and didn't appear to be contaminated, so he poured some over his hands to wipe away the soil. Madison did the same.

Colton wasn't stalling, but he wasn't sure how Madison would react to his response. Colton had adopted a survival mind-set. His will to survive had become tantamount, which meant he removed emotions from his decision making. He needed to make sure Madison was thinking that way also.

"With her home vacant, it's a prime target for others to rummage through," replied Colton. "Mrs. Abercrombie has departed, but she can still help us survive."

Madison looked at the grave and back towards the house. She was apparently wrestling with the notion of going through Mrs. Abercrombie's belongings.

"You're right," said Madison. "I don't like this, Colton. I don't know if I can ever get used to taking other people's things. But if we don't, somebody else will, which might make them stronger and our family more vulnerable."

"Unfortunately, that's the way we have to look at it," said Colton as he embraced Madison. "We're doing this for Alex, and us."

They entered the den and adjusted their eyes to the darkness. The opening of the windows helped ventilate the house, but the air remained barely breathable. Using their flashlights pointed toward the floor, they each went their separate ways. Madison was assigned the kitchen and pantry area while Colton started upstairs.

After opening the windows to allow further ventilation, Colton began to search the bedrooms. He emptied a basket full of books and filled it with medications and toiletries. There were several medical devices, including a blood pressure kit, an arm sling, and two mercury-in-glass thermometers.

In Mrs. Abercrombie's bedroom, Colton paused to study the photographs of her deceased husband on the wall. He was a decorated Vietnam War veteran. The pictures showed him in his dress uniform, as well as various candid images with his platoon. A folded United States flag was respectfully placed on a small table under the wall display. Colton took it and muttered, "I'll find a good spot for this, sir."

On her dresser stood a vintage radio, which operated on vacuum tubes. Colton shined his light on the back and found an identification plate that read Emerson Model 126. He decided to give it a try when they returned home. Colton set the flag next to it.

"Colton, are you almost finished?" Madison asked in a loud whisper from downstairs.

"Yeah, just another few minutes," he replied. "I'm almost done up here."

He looked through her nightstand drawer and found a loaded handgun and a box of forty-five caliber bullets. He illuminated the weapon and studied it. He immediately went back to the images and studied one of Mr. Abercrombie's photos. It was the same weapon. This was Mr. Abercrombie's sidearm from his days in the service over forty years ago. *Thank you, sir.*

Colton and Madison finished going through the home and only took what they needed. In addition to the significant amount of canned vegetables, soups, and meats, Mrs. Abercrombie had a lot of baking ingredients and spices. Her kitchen cupboards were stocked like someone who only ate out once a month. As Colton and Madison left, they thanked Mrs. Abercrombie for adding a week's worth of food to the Rymans' survival pantry and said one more prayer for her.

Chapter 20

DAY SIX
11:00 a.m., September 14
Ryman Residence
Belle Meade, Tennessee

Colton stared down Harding Place, a usually busy thoroughfare that was now deserted. He contemplated whether people were hiding behind locked doors, occasionally peering through their curtains in fear of every unusual sound. Oddly, yet fortunately, he hadn't heard gunfire the last few nights. With the darkness, came silence and sound carried easily now, Despite this new normal, except for the occasional raised voices and barking dogs, it was eerily quiet. In his gut, Colton felt things were about to change—for the worse.

As Americans began to accept the permanency of the loss of power, citizens around the country began to demand answers and protested to exhibit their displeasure. Shock and disbelief had been replaced with anger and frustration.

Alex had successfully found two ham radio operators who were broadcasting news from around the country. At first, people found their way to the FEMA and National Guard installations and protested. After a few days of ineffectual demands, the protestors realized demonstrations were not the answer. Their government had failed them, and they knew it.

The citizens began to take the recovery process into their own hands. Riots were breaking out in the large population areas, and looting was rampant. Most population centers in excess of ten thousand people became a war zone.

Nashville was no different, which accounted for the lack of a military presence in their neighborhood. Colton did not think the Guard had the personnel to enforce the President's martial law directives, but he was concerned that the pounding on the front door could come at any time. In the name of fairness and equality, the government could sentence his family to death by taking their food. This weighed on him all the time.

"Hey, mister, I'd offer a penny for your thoughts, but a penny is truly worthless now, I suspect." Madison laughed as she joined Colton on the sidewalk. She knocked him on the noggin. "Everything okay in there? Sounds hollow to me."

"Ha-ha." Colton laughed. He turned and hugged his wife a little tighter than normal. "You don't seem concerned about this HPA meeting."

"We've got nothing to be ashamed of," she responded. "I am glad the Kaplans and Youngs are going with us. So what were you thinking about?"

"Knock on wood, but the apocalypse has been too quiet."

"I don't know if I'd agree with that necessarily," said Madison. "Let me see. We've buried three of our neighbors. We've been confronted by the HPA, resulting in an armed standoff. My husband and daughter sneak out of the house at night to rummage through the neighbors' kitchen pantries. That doesn't sound *quiet* to me."

Colton laughed and looked for their escorts to the HPA meeting. Glancing at his watch, he realized it was still early, which also gave them a few more minutes to talk. With their newly acquired weapons, Colton needed to broach the subject of using them.

"I need to talk with you about something without Alex around," started Colton. "We've tried to fly under the radar here, but that has never been our forte. Despite our best efforts, we'll draw the attention of people with ill intent. Unfortunately, I'm afraid the fight will come to us."

"I think you've done a great job of fortifying our home and setting up an around-the-clock patrol as part of our routine."

"That's only part of the issue," continued Colton. "We have to be prepared to defend our family, with force if necessary. Where do we draw the line on violence?"

"*This far you may come and no farther*," replied Madison, quoting Job. "The sea has its limits, and so should we."

"Okay, but we should agree upon how far we'll let someone push us before we decide that action, in the form of shooting at them, is appropriate. The time to decide is not in the heat of the moment."

Colton turned to Madison and placed her hands on the Taurus tucked in his waistband. "Look at me. I'm carrying a gun, in the open, in the middle of Harding Place, and it doesn't even seem abnormal."

"It's necessary now."

"I agree," replied Colton. "But how do we decide if it's necessary to use it?"

Madison abruptly turned as she realized Alex was coming out of the house. She finished her thought. "Here's what I think. Look at a gun as a car horn. You don't use it out of anger to express displeasure with another's actions. You use it to warn of the consequences of their actions. Someone shoots at us. We shoot back. If they point their gun at us, we may shoot first because we can't take any chances. We live in a world without laws but are still governed by our morals and beliefs. But the operable word in that sentence now is *live*. We *live*, Colton, no matter what it requires us to do."

Alex saw them and approached cautiously. "You guys look serious," said Alex. "Everything okay?"

"Yes, honey," replied Madison. "We are worried about you going to see the Holder boy again."

"It'll be fine. He's harmless, and you guys will have your hands full with his stepdad. I should be worried about y'all."

"Don't take any chances, Alex," said Colton. "I don't trust those people. Holder is potentially dangerous. Jimmy sounds like a good kid, clearly the opposite of his stepdad. But tell him you can only stay for an hour, and then you have to come home. Got it?"

"Yes, Daddy," she replied, and then gave them both a kiss on the cheek.

Colton was a positive influence in Alex's life. He provided her a consistent presence and level demeanor. The emotions of an adolescent girl could result in ups and downs. Colton saw the effect this had on Alex and Madison's relationship. Alex treated her mother differently. Their conversations were sometimes complicated by the delicate relationships that often existed between mothers and teenage daughters. Madison looked at Alex as an extension of herself. Alex, on the other hand, strived for individuality and independence.

Like any human relationship, there was compromise required. She and Colton agreed that if Madison were to fight Alex on every issue, there would never be peace. They learned the heated conflicts of one day would become insignificant the next. Madison sought to be the adult in the room and allowed Alex her voice, even if she didn't agree with it at times.

Colton wondered if he could apply that same reasoning to the first time someone pointed a gun at him.

CHAPTER 21

DAY SIX
Noon, September 14
HPA Meeting House
Trimble Rd. & Lynnwood Blvd.
Belle Meade, Tennessee

As their group of six walked onto the vacant lot across from the HPA meeting house, the whispers began.

She waited 'til the bruises went away to show her face.

Look, she can't even walk next to him.

He's scowling—typical abusive husband.

Madison noticed it first and mentioned it to Karen Kaplan. Their women's intuition seemed to take over, probably from years of experience in dealing with complicated social situations.

Ostracism caused real pain because it thwarted our basic needs for belonging, self-esteem, and control. It had become the number one tool of bullies and cowards. The ability to physically lash out at one another was against the law, so people found a way to torture each other mentally. It was part of school life for children and social media for people of all ages. Madison perceived it to be on full display today, but she was ready for them.

"Welcome, everyone," said Wren to a consistently dwindling crowd. "I wanna start out today's meeting with some good news. We've learned FEMA will be setting up a temporary food and water distribution center at Belle Meade Country Club. It will open up at eight in the morning. I'd like to encourage everyone to be there bright and early to get your share of the supplies. I also expect our government officials will be there to provide us an update regarding the restoration of power."

A woman in the crowd shouted a question. "What about the fire that's been burning to our west near the interstate? Isn't the country club a little close to that?"

"Great question," responded Wren. "I haven't confirmed this. Thus my answer is clearly speculative, but I believe the Nashville Electric substation caught on fire. Without a functioning fire department, it has been burning out of control and spreading throughout the area near the interstate. I'll try to get more on that tomorrow."

"What about the looting in our neighborhood?" asked a woman, who Madison recognized as living half a mile down Harding Place toward 100 Oaks. "The Moultries' home was broken into last night. I made a point to put it on the list at the first HPA meeting, and it was still looted. How could this happen?"

"Let me take that one, Shane," said Gene Andrews. "Ma'am, we've tried to organize patrols to canvas the entire area, but we're short on volunteers. I'm sorry about what happened to their home, but without the warm bodies, it's impossible to protect every vacant property."

The neighbor persisted. "I don't understand. We've volunteered to help out, and we've given you extra food. Shouldn't that entitle us to be watched over first?"

Wren took the lead in the conversation and began to answer, but glared at the Ryman contingent first. "Again, ma'am, I'm sorry. Of course we appreciate the sacrifices that you and so many of our neighbors have made. The President asked us to help one another until help arrived or power was restored. Some good people, like yourself, have complied. But, sadly, there are a selfish few who choose to reap the benefits of our good deeds and not contribute to the well-being of all of us."

Madison cringed as the angry shouts came from all around them. People were frustrated with the lack of action on the part of FEMA and the HPA, and they were looking for a target.

"That's not fair!"

"Why not?"

"If they're not putting something in, why should we?"

"Yeah!"

"They've got a lot of nerve! Who are they?"

Wren raised his hand to calm the crowd. He set his jaw and spoke. "As a matter of fact, there is someone among us today who has the ability to power the appliances we need to store and cook food. He could help charge the batteries we need to power our critical medical devices. But he has determined that his needs are more important than helping all of us!"

"Who is it?"

"Step forward, you selfish bast—!"

"Enough!" shouted Colton. Madison had known Colton for most of her adult life and she'd never seen him approach a situation like this angrily. "It's true. I do have a—"

"Of course, it's the wife beater!" shouted one woman.

"You're the guy. You've gotta lot of nerve showing up here."

"Christie told us what you did. You should be ashamed!" shouted another woman.

Rusty Kaplan stepped up to defend Colton. "You people are all wrong and need to pipe down! I've been the Rymans' next-door neighbor for many years and know for a fact that he would never raise a hand to Madison or their daughter. In fact, he was out of town when this—"

"Who can believe you?"

"You're his friend, of course you'd lie!"

"Did he bribe you with the generator to lie for him?"

The crowd was becoming hostile, and they were closing around Madison and the others. She hooked her arm under Colton's and noticed he had his hand on the gun.

Rusty continued. "It's not a lie. I saw the whole thing on the news. She was attacked—"

The crowd burst out in spontaneous laughter as they mocked Kaplan's statement.

"Very funny! The whole thing happened to be on the six o'clock news."

"Yeah, and none of us can confirm it, now can we?"

The crowd pressed closer, and Madison became frightened, then angry. She'd hoped this wasn't necessary.

"Shut up! All of you shut up! My husband didn't hit me, he loves me. This was a nasty vicious rumor started by Christie Wren and her husband. I have proof!"

Madison reached into her jeans pocket and pulled out Alex's fully charged iPhone, which had been stored in the Faraday cage. She had the downloaded video cued up and pushed play. The crowd became quiet in amazement at the functioning telephone. The video played the news report, and the images of her being beaten were seen by nearly everyone in the crowd.

Madison had vindicated her husband. But he was cleared of only one charge, as she quickly learned.

"Okay, big deal. How did you get your cell phone to work?"

"Can you make a call?"

"Do you have Internet access?"

Madison was shocked. She looked at Colton and her friends. She thought this would put an end to the whole ordeal. As a result, she wasn't surprised to see Wren take advantage of the situation.

"You see? This is what I'm talking about. Ryman has valuable resources that he refuses to share with his neighbors in need. Do any of you have a functioning cell phone?"

"Nooooo!" the crowd roared its displeasure.

"It doesn't function. It simply—" Madison's attempt at an explanation was drowned out by Wren's bellowing.

"I ask you, fellow neighbors, if this is fair?"

"Noooooo!"

"I agree," continued Wren. "Ryman, I'm calling on you to do the right thing and share the wealth. Provide us access to the things that will help this community survive. If you won't, then don't attend our meetings and don't look to us for help!"

CHAPTER 22

DAY SIX
5:00 p.m., September 14
Ryman Residence
Belle Meade, Tennessee

Alex cleared the table of the paper plates and plastic cutlery. The sounds of clanking dishes being piled into the sink following a meal was replaced with a quick, easy cleanup into a lawn and leaf bag in the corner of the kitchen. The vase of freshly picked flowers normally in the center of the table was replaced with three handguns, one for each of the Rymans.

"Did Jimmy give you a hard time about requesting another gun?" asked Colton.

"No, but sorry, Mom, I had to throw you under the bus a little bit," replied Alex.

"What? How?"

"I told Jimmy you didn't approve of the gun and took it away from me," she replied. "He gave me this one just like it. More ammo too."

"Okay, are we done with this undercover operation now?" asked Madison.

"Just one more, Mom. I want to get one of those AR-15s. Jimmy showed me how it works. They're really neat."

"Great! Neat," said Madison sarcastically.

"Plus, it gives me time just to talk," said Alex. "Today, he told me about his real dad, who lives in Antioch."

"Does he spend time with his father?" asked Colton.

"Only once a month," he replied. "His dad lost his job a long time ago and never got back on his feet. Jimmy thinks he felt guilty for not being able to take care of him, which is why his dad allowed Mr. Holder to adopt him. Jimmy didn't care about *stuff.* He just wanted to spend time with his dad."

Alex sat quietly for a moment as she thought about Jimmy's predicament. His mom was probably stuck in Washington, D.C. indefinitely, and his real father in Antioch was nearly fifteen miles away, which might as well be Washington.

"It's tough on Jimmy, you know?" started Alex. "His only family is a man who doesn't know how to care for him and throws him some silly gift once in a while like you'd give a dog a leftover soup bone."

"I feel sorry for him," said Madison. "I'd love to have him over for a meal, although canned soup isn't most people's favorite. It's just too dangerous, honey."

Alex sighed. "I know, Mom. Really, he enjoys having me as a friend. He needs somebody to talk to. His stepdad is gone all the time, even at night sometimes. He's always down at the HPA house."

"Don't we know it," said Colton.

Alex continued. "This morning, he was in a pretty good mood because his stepdad left him a present. It was a military jacket with patches on it and everything."

Madison turned to Colton and asked, "Isn't Holder a banker? He doesn't seem like the military type."

Colton shrugged and was about to answer when Alex spoke up. "No. Jimmy said his stepdad got it from one of the neighbors. I guess people have been helping them out with food and stuff. Jimmy said the people wanted to thank Mr. Holder for watching over their place, so they gave him the jacket. I think their name was Mule-tree or something like that."

Colton and Madison simultaneously sat up in their chairs and asked, "Moultrie?"

Alex was puzzled and responded, "That's it. Moultrie. Do you know them?"

Colton immediately peppered her with questions. "What else did he say?"

"Jimmy said his stepdad, Mr. Wren, and Mr. Andrews were helping out in the neighborhood by watching over everything. Because it was most dangerous at night, they patrol the streets, watching for looters."

"Did Jimmy say where they patrol?" asked Colton.

"Not really. Well, he did say they pay special attention to the homes that are vacant. You know, to protect them."

"Yeah, I bet," said Madison sarcastically.

"Did you notice anything else different about their home from the last time you were over there?" asked Colton.

Alex thought for a moment. There was something. "Oh, yeah. I used to come and go through the garage. In fact, the garage door was always rolled open. Today, the car was rolled out into the driveway, and the door was closed."

"Was it like that yesterday?" asked Colton.

"Yes, as a matter of fact, it was. I remember asking Jimmy why I couldn't leave through the garage. He said his stepdad locked the double dead bolt on the garage door to keep their stuff safe. That's so weird because Mr. Holder has all of those guns in the basement, and he isn't worried about someone going down there."

Madison leaned back in her chair and looked at Colton. "He's hiding something."

"Here's what they're doing, Maddie," started Colton. "At the HPA meetings, Wren encourages the neighbors to provide the street addresses of those homes that are abandoned. At night, under the guise of patrolling the neighborhood, they break in and steal what they want. The Moultries' home was last night's target."

"They're hiding everything in Holder's garage."

"Daddy, Jimmy doesn't have anything to do with that," said Alex. Jimmy had confided in her that Holder had beat him before. She didn't want to tell her dad because he had enough to worry about. "I don't want him to get in trouble."

"We understand, honey," said Madison. "Don't worry."

Colton stood up and walked through the kitchen as the light began to fade. He and Alex were supposed to go to the O'Malleys' that evening.

"Daddy, what's wrong?"

"I was trying to figure out how they were getting around," said Colton.

"The phony guardsmen," interjected Madison.

"Yes! They're in cahoots together. Wren, Andrews, and Holder are gathering the addresses and then feeding the information to those guys. They have an operating truck and a perfect cover."

"And guns," added Madison. "Nobody would dare confront them."

Alex and Madison sat quietly, allowing Colton to think it through. Finally, Colton spoke up.

"I need some kind of proof. Wren and company are using this as an opportunity to line their pockets. They're giving our neighbors false hope by day and stealing from them at night."

"Daddy, are we going to the O'Malleys' tonight? It's getting dark."

"No. After today, we need to double our night watch."

CHAPTER 23

DAY SEVEN
2:00 p.m., September 15
Ryman Residence
Belle Meade, Tennessee

By day seven, Madison had cooked all the foods stored in their refrigerator and freezer. Colton drained the gasoline out of the generator. He turned his focus to topping off the Wagoneer's gas tank. If an unforeseen event forced them to flee their home, he wanted a full tank for the journey. The empty cans gave him the ability to siphon fuel out of lawn equipment around the neighborhood or stalled vehicles. He decided to practice on the dead Suburban.

Colton had already emptied the truck of its contents, including the floor mats and tire-changing tools. He tried to clean up the Wagoneer and get the smell of dead animal out of it. After a lot of Febreze, the Jeep was tolerable. The O'Malleys had a rack that slid into the trailer hitch receiver. It was large enough to hold the generator and four gas cans. Colton attached it to the hitch and loaded up the generator. Now, he planned on filling the four five-gallon cans with available gasoline.

The Suburban was perfectly positioned from its crash landing the first day. By running up on the retaining wall, it created plenty of room for Colton to crawl under it. He checked for a drain plug in the fuel tank. Older vehicles had them, but it had been nearly twenty years since he'd worked on a car.

There wasn't one. The next option was to siphon out the gas. The newer gas tanks had protective screens or metal blocking devices to prevent gasoline spillage during an accident. He'd come up with a workaround. While he was loading sandbags from the cable repair site down the street, he'd grabbed several sizes of rigid, underground cable housing to be used for this purpose. First, he crammed a six-foot, quarter-inch plastic line into the gas tank until it hit the blockade. He twisted and pushed, eventually forcing the tube around the metal valve blocking entry to the tank.

Colton removed the flexible hose from their small sump pump, which was used to remove standing water from their pool cover in the winter. He forced it down into the tank until it reached the bottom. This was an extremely slow method of siphoning gas. Colton estimated it took about ten minutes to pull out a gallon of gas. Colton always said time was only worth what you were getting paid for it, and with the value of a gallon of gas being astronomical, it was worth the effort.

While he supervised the siphoning process, several of the residents returned from Belle Meade Country Club where the water and food distribution trucks were set up. Colton slowly felt for his weapon, which had become a habit now. Every human contact was a potential threat.

They were all empty-handed. He didn't recognize any of the faces as being from around his neighborhood. The first two men and a woman passed by without glancing in his direction. They looked defeated. Shuffling their feet as they walked, their heads hung down, and one even appeared to be disoriented. It was hot as blazes again, and the trip to the FEMA trailers was not worth the effort.

Colton was curious, so he forced the conversation. He stepped into the street and stopped two men who were bloodied.

"What happened, guys?"

"It was a bust," replied one of the men. "We got there around midnight last night to get in line. We didn't care about the curfew. We need food and water."

Colton studied their faces. He'd never seen the look of despair before, but now it was looking back at him. "Were there a lot of people there?"

"Several hundred at least," replied the other man, who had an open gash across his cheek. He'd ripped his shirt sleeve off and was dabbing at the wound.

"The first thing that made people mad is they had this roped-off area that we had to walk through to get into the parking lot where the trucks were parked. We were handed this."

Colton took the paper from the man. It read Declaration of Martial Law. He glanced over it and then tried to hand it back to the man.

"You keep it," he said. "Before we could enter the parking lot, we were forced to give up our guns."

"Yeah," started the other man. "They kept shouting to give up all weapons or there wouldn't be any food distributed. This really made people mad. Some tried to leave, but there were plenty of National Guardsmen there. They were taken down, and their guns were confiscated."

"One guy tried to hide his rifle by stuffing it down his pants leg, but another person in line told on him. This caused a fight, and both of them were thrown out of line."

"Other than that, everything was orderly until they opened the trailers up," said the other man. "That's when all heck broke loose."

"For one thing, they were almost an hour late," said the gashed-cheekbone man. "People were angry before the distribution even started. Military guys were standing around, and plenty of folks in neatly pressed FEMA uniforms, but they weren't doin' anything except talking and—"

"Drinking coffee," interrupted the other man.

"What?" asked Colton.

"You heard us. The FEMA people were standing around the trailers guarded by men with guns, drinking coffee right in front of us while we waited for the trailers to open."

Colton shook his head. The government bureaucrats who were part of the FEMA relief effort weren't suffering, apparently.

"What happened when they opened the trailers?" asked Colton.

"One trailer had bottled water, and the other trailer had boxes of food. Each person was allowed twelve pint-sized water bottles and a box of twelve freeze-dried meals."

"I've got my wife and two kids. That would only last us one day!"

Colton once again looked at the dozens of people headed their way from the club. They were all empty-handed.

"Why didn't you get at least that?" asked Colton.

"As the trailer doors opened, the first thing we noticed was that they weren't full. These were big military rigs pulling trailers labeled Sysco. They could've held enough food for everybody, but the trailers were only half full."

"Yeah, that made folks mad from the git-go. The people to the rear of us started pushing forward. Others noticed the surge and then bum-rushed the trailers. It was a mass of people trampling and crushing everyone in their path."

"My gosh!" exclaimed Colton. A family of four stopped to join the conversation. The children seemed to be very weak.

"The military guys tried to get things under control, and a few folks got some supplies. Then the FEMA people made it worse."

"How so?" asked Colton.

"They treated us like schoolkids," said the woman who had joined the conversation. "The head FEMA guy grabbed one of those megaphones and began to yell for us to get into a single file line or they were going to close the doors and leave."

"Yeah, that's exactly what he said. It made it worse because then people panicked. I've never seen anything like it. People had no regard for their fellow human being."

The woman started crying. "My kids were being trampled. The army guys pulled out these black batons and started beating people down. There was blood everywhere." She was sobbing at this point, and her husband tried to comfort her, but she just pushed him away.

"Did it ever get under control?" asked Colton.

"No. They closed up the doors, just like the FEMA guy said, and they all left. People chased them for a while. Some were throwing rocks. It looked like a scene from Iraq."

"You wanna know the worst part?" asked the woman. Then she

answered herself, "We didn't learn anything. The FEMA people wouldn't answer our questions. There was no announcement of when the power would be restored. They didn't say when they would be back. All we got was that piece of paper with a list of new rules and the locations of FEMA camps."

The woman took her kids by the hands and began to walk away. Her husband followed them, as did the other two men. Colton looked westward down Harding Place. Dozens more were headed his way.

Colton pondered and realized how lucky his family was. It had only been seven days since the solar flare, and people were growing more desperate. Respect for others was gone. His neighbors were impoverished, having burned through the contents of their kitchen cupboards already. With no place to turn, these people put all of their hopes in FEMA and the National Guard. Their government, however, left them bloodied and mentally broken.

CHAPTER 24

DAY EIGHT
1:00 a.m., September 16
Ryman Residence
Belle Meade, Tennessee

Sitting on the front porch with the shotgun laid across his lap, Colton couldn't get the scene from that afternoon out of his mind. The Great Depression that hit America in the 1930s was an example of a national economic collapse. As in any catastrophic event, fingers of blame were quickly pointed. Some economists opined a lack of government control and intervention left the free market unable to sustain itself. Others believed government over-regulation and manipulation was the problem. Overall, politicians and pundits were convinced the economy was capable of correcting itself unless a catastrophic event occurred—a trigger event, which forced an already unstable economic climate over the edge.

The collapse of the nation's power grid following the solar flare was America's trigger event. Colton conjured up images of the Great Depression. One photograph came to mind of a hungry and desperate mother who, with her young children, were living off vegetables from surrounding farms and the crows they were able to kill. The picture, which became famously known as *Migrant Mother*, was embedded in Colton's mind as he recalled the day's events.

During the Great Depression, people helped one another. Families pooled their resources, and the church became a place of refuge and a provider of sustenance. Colton continued to wrestle with whether he should share his family's food with others. He was a generous, giving man. *But how could he face his dying family, knowing he gave away the food they needed to live another day?* When feelings of guilt popped into his mind, he thought of the *Migrant Mother. I will not let that happen to Madison and Alex.*

He sat quietly, listening to the faint bark of a dog in the distance. After a week, his eyes had grown accustomed to seeing in the dark. He was able to detect movement better. His ears became attuned to unusual sounds. Gunshots in the distance became more prevalent, especially from the direction of downtown Nashville.

It was against this quiet backdrop that Colton heard the clanking of cans followed by hushed voices coming from the backyard. He bolted off the porch, adrenaline rushing through his body, preparing him for a fight-or-flight reaction to a potential threat.

His eyes darted in every direction. *Did he hear correctly? Was he too deep in thought to comprehend the noise?*

Colton cautiously rounded the corner of the house and approached the gate entering the pool area—trying to stay low to the ground. He'd left it open during his evening rounds and immediately got upset with himself for providing intruders easy access to his backyard.

CRACK!

Colton heard the crunch of a twig in the trees behind the house. Someone was sneaking through the woods!

SHHHH!

More than one person. Colton moved into the patio area, remaining in a low crouch. He glanced up at his daughter's window. Had she heard it too? He had no way to warn Madison and Alex without being discovered.

The people who were approaching his home through the backyard had tripped one of the makeshift alarms farthest from the house. Colton had set it up as a deterrent. He hoped any potential marauder would hear the alarm they stumbled upon, realize they were detected, and then leave.

They were still coming—bold, unafraid, and thus, dangerous.

Colton immediately ran a thousand things through his head. *How many are there? Will the girls be safe? Do I yell and warn them away?* This didn't appear to be a time for negotiation. These people were up to no good. *Do I shoot first and ask questions later?*

This last thought forced Colton to think about the readiness and use of his weapon. He was unsure how to use the various shotgun shells purchased by Madison. He'd studied the three options and determined that the birdshot held the most pellets and would be the most forgiving if his aim was off. Then, the buckshot only held nine pellets and would be more lethal. Finally, he decided the slugs could be used for hunting or when he became a better shot. With this in mind, he'd staggered his rounds—one birdshot followed by a buckshot shell and so on, for a total of five.

Only five! Once again, Colton closed his eyes and shook his head. He was about to enter into a possible gunfight with only five shotgun shells. The others were hidden inside the house.

RATTLE, RATTLE, RATTLE was followed by a loud whisper, but close enough for Colton to hear. The perimeter alarm closest to the trail entering the clearing was tripped. He had to make a decision.

Colton was completely unprepared for a gunfight. If these people were heavily armed or if they had the numbers, their home would be overrun and his entire family might be killed. He had no choice. He had to be the aggressor.

Colton flipped off the safety and pointed the Remington into the woods. There was no discernible target. None of the intruders had reached the opening, which was just sixty feet from his position. He quickly glanced up at Alex's window to see if there was any sign of her or Madison. *They must be sleeping, but not for long.*

He took aim at the funnel point he'd created where the trail emptied into their yard, and gently squeezed the trigger.

BOOM!

The retort of the Remington 870 rang in his ears and reverberated off the walls of the pool house and the garage. The echo was probably heard for miles. The recoil pushed into his shoulder, knocking him back against the fence.

ARRRGGGGHHH!

A man was screaming in pain in the woods.

"Are you okay, Gene?"

Before he could answer, a barrage of gunfire streamed out of Alex's window. *They were awake!* Bullets fired wildly into the trees, splintering bark and hitting the ground with a thug.

"ARRRGGGGHHH! I'm hit!" Two wounded.

CRACK! CRACK! CRACK!

Crap! Return fire! This time the bullets were flying over his head and hitting the roof of the garage, causing him to dive for cover behind the retaining wall. This gave Colton a clear view into Alex's window. In unison, from each side of the window, Madison and Alex stuck their hands out and opened fire on the woods. The bullets missed their mark, this time shredding the tops of the trees. But the deluge had the desired effect.

"Run!" shouted one of the men.

One of the wounded intruders was still groaning.

"Somebody help him," said a new voice. Colton counted at least four or five voices now.

Then, Colton heard a sixth, somewhat recognizable voice. "Let's finish what we started!"

CRACK! CRACK! CRACK!

This time, the bullets hit the back of the house, with one shattering the boarded-up window in the study. Alex shrieked.

They weren't going to back down! This was life or death now. Colton pulled the slide on the shotgun and inserted another round into the chamber. He quickly rose up onto his knees and, using the retaining wall as cover, blindly fired the double-ought buck shell into the woods.

BOOM!

"UGGGGHHH!" Another hit.

Madison and Alex fired again until Colton heard the *click-click-click* of their emptied weapons. He racked another round and got ready. They were down to three shots left. He waited. He had to be accurate now.

"C'mon. Run. Everybody. RUN!" The shouts of retreat streamed from the dark woods. The alarms were tripped once again. Cracking twigs and screams of pain filled the air. Within thirty seconds, everything was quiet. *But is it over?*

Chapter 25

DAY EIGHT
Noon, September 16
HPA Meeting House
Trimble Rd. & Lynnwood Blvd.
Belle Meade, Tennessee

Colton hadn't slept. After the gunfight he ran upstairs to check on Madison and Alex. He positioned them on opposite sides of the house and warned them to stay still. He had been unsure whether the attack was over and vowed not to be surprised again.

"Colton, did you not sleep?" asked Bill Young as he approached Colton on the sidewalk. He was carrying a suitcase, as was his wife. Colton was puzzled.

"Well, as you guys undoubtedly heard, it was a busy night," replied Colton.

Diane spoke up. "Colton, we're not cut out for this, and frankly, we're amazed we made it this long. What happened last night was eye-opening for us."

"I'm sorry, you guys," said Colton. "There were at least five or six men coming to rob us or worse."

"Hey, hey," interrupted Bill, trying to reassure Colton. "This is not just about last night, although what happened was the impetus for our decision. We're almost out of food and things to drink. We've been out of fresh water for days, and we've resorted to drinking sodas and fruit juices."

"Our meals consist of canned peaches and the juice that it contains," said Diane.

As if to drive the point home, Bill hitched up his pants to keep them from falling off him. He reached into his pocket and handed Colton his keys.

"What's this?" asked Colton.

"We're walking to the FEMA camp at 100 Oaks Mall," replied Bill. "Vandy Hospital used to operate medical facilities there, and we think they can use people like us. We're sure other refugees are having difficulty coping. Our thought is we could trade our psychologist services to the government in exchange for room and board."

"Just until the power comes back on, of course," added Diane.

Colton looked at the Youngs and realized they'd resigned their fate to FEMA. Bill and Diane always espoused the *cradle-to-grave* approach of the U.S. government. It appeared the Youngs were turning over the final stretch of their lives to the benefactor who, despite warnings, failed to prepare for this catastrophe.

"Colton, if you don't mind, please watch over our home for us," said Bill. "You're welcome to anything we have that might be useful. Help yourself."

"Yes, by all means," added Diane. "There isn't much food left, but Madison might be able to work with some of my other things."

The Kaplans joined them on the sidewalk and chatted for a moment. They finally said their goodbyes, and the Youngs held hands as they wheeled their suitcases down the street toward the east. If it were an airport, they'd resemble a loving couple heading toward their departure gate for a vacation. Today, they were just *departing*.

Colton tried to steady his nerves as he entered the HPA meeting house. Because of the continuously shrinking crowds, Wren had moved the meeting back inside the sunroom. The combination of adrenaline, instant coffee, and anger put Colton on edge. Another confrontation was coming, and he was ready.

Wren and Holder took their customary positions at the front of the room. Colton, however, did not attempt to blend into the middle of the crowd this time. He stood front and center, immediately staring down the leaders of the HPA.

Wren made an opening statement about the FEMA camp at 100

Oaks and encouraged people to consider this option if their supplies were running out. Wren asked them to make a note of their decision to leave on today's clipboard being circulated. *Naturally*, thought Colton.

Colton continued to stare a hole through Wren and Holder. Holder finally picked up on this and nudged Wren while whispering into his ear.

"Ryman, nice of you to join us," started Wren sarcastically. "You got something on your mind?"

"Yeah, I do!" Colton said with a raised voice. "I wanna know who attacked my house last night!" The people in the room began to whisper among themselves, but Colton waited patiently for a reaction from Holder in particular. Holder returned the glare and stood stoic.

"How would we know, Ryman?" replied Wren. "But it should come as no surprise to anyone in this room. We asked you to contribute to the well-being of your neighborhood, and you refused. You are the type of hoarder the President has condemned, and you're lucky it wasn't the National Guard knocking on your door."

"At least they'd come in the daylight and to our front door," Colton shot back. He directed his attention at Holder now. "I mean, what kind of coward lurks through the woods to attack a man, his wife, and young daughter? The same type of coward who brings four or five men with him, firing guns at us."

"If they did, Ryman, it was your own selfishness that brought this on," said Wren. "You should've put the needs of everyone on an equal footing with your own."

"Shut up!" screamed Colton. "You're not going to blame me for someone trying to attack my family!"

The entire room was talking among themselves, and Colton saw Rusty Kaplan move to his side. Rusty whispered to Colton, attempting to diffuse the situation, but Colton was not interested.

He continued. "Where's Gene Andrews today?" Colton was shouting. "Is he pullin' shotgun pellets out of his cowardly—"

"You need to calm down, Ryman," said Holder, the veins popping out of his red face and forehead. "Calm down or else—"

"Or else what, Holder?" asked Colton. "You gonna finish off the job? Where were you last night around one a.m.?"

Holder didn't respond, but his body language said it all. He was now nervous because he was implicated. The crowd began to mumble louder.

"What about it, Holder?" questioned Colton. He took a step closer to Holder and placed his hand on his hip next to his nine millimeter. "Do me a favor, would ya? Repeat these words for me so everyone in this room can hear—let's finish what we started."

A hush came over the room as Holder broke eye contact and looked into the backyard. Was he eyeing an escape route?

"Say it, Holder," shouted Colton. "Say the words—let's finish what we started!"

Nobody spoke a word while Colton waited for his answer. He wasn't going to let them off the hook.

Finally, Wren spoke first. "Listen, Ryman. Everybody here is sorry for what you went through. We're all glad your family wasn't hurt, and I'm sure it won't happen again. This is a time for all of us to pull together, not make accusations that will tear us apart."

Colton thought for a moment, but he wasn't naïve. Wren's hollow words weren't going to deter him from the task at hand. He was going to blow this whole thing up.

"That's a load of crap, Wren, and you know it!" yelled Colton. He turned to the rest of the homeowners, many of whom stepped back in fear. *Good.*

"By a show of hands, how many of you have received food from Wren and the HPA?"

Two people raised their hands out of forty.

"Again, by a show of hands, how many of your friends' vacant homes have been broken into?"

A third of the room raised their hands this time. The attendees looked at one another and erupted into chatter.

"Ryman!" shouted Wren, attempting to regain control of the meeting. "That's enough! Everybody, please, settle down."

Colton ignored Wren and continued—this time louder. "All of

you who raised your hands, did this happen before or after you notified the HPA that the homes were vacant?"

"After."

"After."

People began to look at each other. The response was repeated.

"After."

"After."

"After."

"Definitely after."

Colton nodded his head and smiled. Now his neighbors saw the pattern. He made his closing argument.

"You've been doing their job for them," said Colton, pointing with his thumb over his shoulder toward Wren and Holder. "You tell them which homes are vacant and therefore safe to break into. They, or their friends the phony National Guardsmen who were here the other day, break in and steal valuables and food from the people they promised to protect."

"Whadya mean *phony*?" asked Rusty.

"They're not guardsmen," replied Colton. "I suspected something the day they attended the meeting out front. Their uniforms were mismatched. Their boots were not military issue, and their demeanor was undisciplined. They're opportunists posing as our military. Nobody would suspect them of looting."

"How do you know for sure?" asked a man in the rear of the room.

"I saw them leaving a house down the street from me—in broad daylight," replied Colton. "Their old pickup truck was full of clothing, furniture, and paintings. Wren, Andrews, and Holder gave them the perfect cover. They probably meet up here at night and divide up the stolen property. They hoard the food and medicine for themselves while all of you suffer!"

Colton saw it in their faces. They were with him now. He swung around to confront Wren and Holder, but he didn't have to. The shouts from the room were full of hostility.

"Whaddya have to say for yourselves?"

"How could you do this to us?"

"We trusted you!"

"Did you really attack this man and his family in the middle of the night?"

Colton and the others were now silent, as all eyes were on Wren and Holder.

Holder reacted first. He threw his arms up in the air and pushed his way through the crowd toward the screen door leading to the backyard. "I don't need this. I'm outta here!"

"Wait! Answer the man's questions!" A couple of people reached for his arm as he pushed open the door, but Holder evaded their grasp and stormed off. All the attention turned to Wren.

"What about this, Shane?" asked a woman from the back of the room. "Are you a part of this?"

Wren held his hands up and attempted to provide a response. Wren was being bombarded with questions, and he tried to lie his way through it or avoid answering altogether. He was squirming and there was no way out.

Colton had enough, and he was tired. He gradually slid backward through the crowd. As he did, a few people patted him on the back and thanked him. They wished his family well. All Colton could do was smile and nod. His work was done here—for today.

CHAPTER 26

DAY NINE
Noon, September 17
Holder Residence
Belle Meade, Tennessee

"Colton, are you sure this is a good idea?" asked Madison. She tucked her handgun into her waistband. Alex realized for the first time that her entire family was armed as they started their day. "Not only did you knock down the proverbial hornet's nest, but you also kicked it several times as well."

"Now more than ever," replied Colton. "We've got to keep a finger on the pulse of the community. We've got to appear unfazed by yesterday's events. Not being shy of another fight is the best way to exude strength and confidence."

"What do you think will happen?" asked Alex.

"I don't know for sure, honey," replied Colton. "Our biggest priority is protecting ourselves and our home. Keeping apprised of the neighbors' attitudes will allow us to make adjustments when it comes to our security. If the situation is hostile, we may have to consider our alternatives to staying here."

"Leave?" asked Madison. "But I thought, well, I just thought we could make it work here."

Alex instantly became concerned as well. "Daddy, where would we go?"

"I'm not saying we have to go anywhere. I really don't know. But we have to consider the possibility, especially with the change in demeanor of our neighbors. Desperation has reached a fever pitch. Families are showing signs of dehydration. Some have dysentery, which expedites the dehydration process."

Madison interrupted. "Yesterday, I stopped a man and his wife from coming on our property. They asked if we had a pool because they needed water and wanted to take a bath. They didn't beg for food. They wanted to go swimming."

"Daddy, how would we survive on the road? I mean, isn't it dangerous out there?"

Colton gave Alex a hug. "Yes, it is. But it's become increasingly unsafe here. Even though the numbers are dropping, we're still in one of the twenty-five largest cities in America. That's a lot of people who are potential threats. At least in the country, the population is much smaller."

Alex gave him a kiss on the cheek as he pulled away and headed toward the kitchen door. Madison joined him and gave Alex instructions. "Honey, we want you to stay here today."

"But, Mom, Jimmy is expecting me to come over. I want to try to—"

"Alex, please. Listen to your mother," interrupted Colton. "It's too risky now. People could be watching the house, waiting for us to leave. Plus, Holder is really pissed at me. I don't know what he's capable of and I don't want you in his home."

Alex's body slumped into dejection. She wanted to help, and she was being tied down. Her mom returned and gave her a kiss, then whispered, "Okay?"

Alex nodded.

Alex followed her parents outside and watched as they descended the hill towards the Kaplans' house. For several minutes she walked around the house and then looked for any activity up and down their street. It was desolate.

She felt for the keys to the house in her pocket and made a decision. This was probably her last chance to get the gun her family so desperately needed—the AR-15. She would beg Jimmy. She would turn on the waterworks in feigned distress. She would even kiss him if she had to. She was going to get that gun.

Alex quickly locked the door and made her way through the

backwoods to Jimmy's. The garage door was closed as always, but the sliding glass doors entering the den were open. She cautiously approached them and entered the house from the backyard. Something felt—*wrong.*

She didn't call out Jimmy's name as she had during her past visits. Today was different. She might not be welcome. She stuck her head around the corner and looked into the kitchen. Empty. Then she heard muffled voices and a crash that sounded like a box hitting the floor.

The door to the basement was open. Then she heard Jimmy's pleading voice.

"Please! I didn't mean anything by it. Just leave me alone. If you hate me so much, why don't you just let me go?"

"Shut up, you snot-nose little …"

WHACK!

Alex couldn't hear the rest because of Jimmy's wails. He was crying in pain. *What's happening down there?* Alex started to back away from the stairwell to return home.

WHACK!

ARRRRRGGGGGHHHH!

THUMP!

"Please, no more. I'm sorry. Please don't hit me again!" Jimmy was begging for mercy.

WHACK!

Holder was beating Jimmy downstairs. The hackles rose up on Alex's neck, and she pulled her gun. She bounded downstairs—fearless.

What she found in the dimly lit room sickened her. Jimmy was huddled in the far corner of the room, naked except for a pair of boxer shorts. He was curled up in the fetal position with huge bloody welts on his back.

Holder reached back with all his might and swung a studded leather belt down upon Jimmy's back again, drawing more blood.

WHACK!

Alex stood motionless for a moment, unsure of what to do.

Jimmy was sobbing and defenseless. Her trembling hands raised the gun and pointed it at Holder. Jimmy saw Alex and moaned, "Run!"

Holder spun around and stared at Alex. She tried to steady her nerves.

"Who are you?" he bellowed. "What are you doing here? Wait, I know you. You're the Ryman kid. Great. Another brat that needs to be taught a lesson." He started towards her.

"Stop!" shouted Alex.

Holder hesitated when he was twenty feet away and then charged at her.

Law enforcement officers were taught that a suspect armed with a knife or other non-gun weapon and within twenty-one feet presented a deadly threat. The average man could close that twenty-one-foot gap in less than two seconds. In those same two seconds, an officer must recognize the threat, draw, point their weapon, and then pull the trigger.

Alex didn't have law enforcement training, but she did have survival instincts. Her physiological reaction to the threat Holder posed was to stand her ground, squeeze the trigger, and fire.

BOOM!

The sound of the gunshot within the confined space of the basement was deafening. The muzzle blast bounced back at Alex off the four walls. Her ears began to ring as she exhibited the concussive effect from the shot.

Alex tried to focus. Did she shoot Holder? She was partially blinded by the muzzle flash.

"UGH!" groaned Holder. She could hear him on the floor, clawing his way toward her. She couldn't see. *But she could feel him.*

Through the fog that had consumed her senses, she saw him lunge toward her.

"You filthy little b—" he shouted as he grabbed for her ankles.

Alex quickly backed away from him and shot downward. The momentum of the pistol forced her backward, and she fell hard onto the concrete floor. Her head was pounding now, and she couldn't hear. Alex quickly became disoriented.

She barely remembered Jimmy streaking past her and running up the stairs. He didn't stop to help her. He just ran away.

Alex sat there, still pointing the weapon in Holder's direction. He wasn't moving. A rush of air entered the room as Jimmy apparently opened the front door, creating cross ventilation through the house. *Is he going for help? Did he leave me here alone? With Holder? Why isn't he moving?*

Alex's entire body was shaking as she stood, still pointing the gun at Holder's body. She was afraid to get too close, so she picked up a box of ammunition off the workbench and threw it at the body. It hit Holder in the back with an audible *squish* as the bullets splashed into a gaping wound.

No movement or reaction. She grabbed another box, throwing it harder this time and with a little anger attached. *Squish*, followed by the sound of brass rolling around on the floor.

Alex was mad as she shouted at Holder's dead body. "You made me kill you! What's wrong with you? Oh, God!"

Alex collapsed against the workbench for a moment and stared at the body. She began to sob and shake uncontrollably. She tortured herself as she wailed in pain, grief, and anger.

Her head was pounding. Her ears were ringing. Her eyes were blurred from the flashes of light and the unbridled tears.

She'd taken a man's life. She'd taken what God had given to every man and woman.

Then, fifteen-year-old Alex Ryman asked God for forgiveness and thanked him for keeping her alive.

CHAPTER 27

DAY NINE
1:00 p.m., September 17
Holder Residence
Belle Meade, Tennessee

Colton and Madison felt like two kids again as the raindrops began to pelt their faces. It was a welcome relief after two weeks of drought and searing heat. The meeting at the HPA went well. Wren, whose attitude had changed dramatically, was conciliatory and apologetic. The transformation was remarkable in the absence of his cohorts—Andrews and Holder.

As they began the trudge up the driveway, the rain came down harder. Colton actually laughed as they became drenched. The joyous mood quickly ended, however, when he saw his daughter. It was actually Madison who first noticed that something was wrong with Alex. She let go of his hand and ran in a full sprint to the front porch.

Alex sat with her elbows propped on her knees. Her handgun was barely dangling from her fingers. She was completely oblivious to the pouring rain that drenched her body.

Madison took the gun from Alex and set it on the step. She crouched down in front of Alex and moved the wet hair covering her face. Colton studied his daughter's blank, expressionless look. She appeared to be in shock.

"Honey, what's wrong?" asked Madison. "Why are you sitting here like this? Are you okay?"

Alex moved her head in an imperceptible nod. Colton looked around and placed his hand on his weapon. *Was she attacked? Is there someone inside*? He needed to get them out of the rain.

"Maddie, let's get her inside," said Colton, who then turned his attention to Alex. "Come with us, honey. We'll go inside and talk, okay?"

Alex nodded. Colton led them to the kitchen door, eyes darting in all directions for a sign of a threat. He wasn't sure what was wrong with Alex, but he needed to assess their surroundings because she was clearly troubled by something.

Madison led Alex to the sofa, and Colton gave her a bottle of water. After a few sips, Alex broke down in tears. Her emotions poured out as she recounted the events of an hour ago. Madison comforted her daughter while Colton cursed anything and everyone for putting his innocent child into this vicious world.

After Alex calmed down, Colton decided to go to Holder's house. Alex claimed no one heard the shots, but he had to be sure. If there was going to be retribution by Jimmy or the surrounding neighbors, he needed to know about it now so they could plan accordingly.

"I'll be back in a little while," started Colton. "Alex, get some rest. Madison, please be aware that the neighbors may have seen something. Jimmy may show up here. I want you to be vigilant. Okay?"

Madison nodded, wiping away her own tears over the anguish her daughter was suffering. Then Alex stood and adjusted her holster. She picked up the handgun off the table and tucked it into her waistband.

"I'm going with you," Alex announced.

"What? No way," said Colton. "You've been through enough. I won't be—"

"Daddy, it's not safe for you to go alone," said Alex. "Besides, I know my way around the house. It'll be quicker if we go together."

"Alex, please don't relive this whole ordeal," pleaded Madison.

Alex gave her mother a comforting hug. "I'll be fine. C'mon, Daddy, let's get this over with."

Alex turned and exited the living room through the patio doors. Colton shrugged and kissed his wife. He whispered, "I love you," as he pulled away. Madison stood with her arms folded as they left.

The rain had lessened somewhat as the father and daughter wound their way through the wooded trails that connected the backyards of the neighborhood. To their east, the sounds of kids playing outside and a dog barking made the world seem almost normal. But as they arrived at the Holder residence, reality set in.

Colton held his index finger to his lips, encouraging Alex to stay quiet. The two pulled their weapons and entered the den. Colton and Alex moved silently through the first floor, clearing rooms and closets like they'd practiced at home dozens of times. They made their way upstairs and continued the process until they were sure the place was empty.

"Where do you think Jimmy went?" whispered Colton.

"I don't know, Daddy. All he had on were his boxer shorts. He may have grabbed some clothes and left. The other day, he talked about his real father in Antioch. He may have gone there."

Colton approached the stairwell leading to the basement and listened. It was quiet. Once again, he pressed his finger to his lips, followed by an open palm advising Alex to wait upstairs for him.

She shook her head and mouthed the word *no*. He gave her the stern fatherly look like he meant business. She repeated *no*. So they both carefully descended the stairs.

Once at the bottom, Colton determined they were alone except for the dead body of Holder lying in a pool of his own blood and a bed of shiny brass ammunition. He approached the body and stepped on Holder's hand by accident. It startled Colton, but at least he confirmed Holder was dead. He turned to Alex.

"Alex, let's go."

"No way, Dad. It's our turn to finish what I started."

Alex led her dad along the workbench, carefully avoiding the puddle of blood, which stretched six feet away from the body. She reached the back wall and found what she was looking for. She secured her weapon in her pants and reached for an AR-15 off the pegboard wall.

"This is what we need, Daddy," started Alex. Colton holstered his Taurus and took the gun by the handle. This gun did not have a sight attached to it. "Here's another one."

Colton now had two of the Colt Manufacturing AR-15s strapped over his back. Alex pointed out two green military-issue ammo cans weighing twenty to thirty pounds each.

"How do you know these are the right bullets?" asked Colton.

"Jimmy told me this is the proper ammo. The cans also have extra magazines. I just need a couple more things."

Alex rummaged around while Colton looked nervously toward the stairwell. They'd been there too long. A neighbor might show up, or Jimmy might return. Things were too unpredictable right now.

The metallic sound of ammo cans being opened and closed echoed off the walls. Alex was on a mission. Finally, she seemed satisfied and announced, "Let's go."

They stepped gingerly around the body. Colton contemplated burying Holder and cleaning up the mess. Then, he thought against it. If they hadn't been discovered thus far, it would be better to stay as far away from the scene as possible.

As they climbed the stairs, Colton became fully aware that the bodies were just beginning to pile up.

CHAPTER 28

DAY TEN
Noon, September 18
HPA Meeting House
Trimble Rd. & Lynnwood Blvd.
Belle Meade, Tennessee

Colton held hands with Alex as they walked to the HPA meeting. Despite the cooler temperatures following the rain shower, Alex's hands felt clammy. After yesterday's shooting, Colton feared the neighbors would turn against him if Alex's involvement were discovered. Attendance at the meeting gave them the opportunity see if Holder's body had been found and to diffuse an angry reaction.

Outwardly, Alex was not struggling with her decision to shoot Holder. She justified the decision to defend herself. Justification and acceptance, however, are two different things.

Inwardly, her feelings could be suppressed. Shock, sorrow, numbness, anger, and disillusionment were all possible. Colton hoped this would pass over time, but he intended to provide her the care and support she needed to lessen the emotional impact. Ultimately, he hoped Alex's self-reproach over the killing would become more manageable. Unfortunately, death was becoming commonplace.

Colton pulled Alex close and put his arm around her shoulder. "Are you okay, honey?" He wished the Youngs hadn't left for 100 Oaks. Their expertise would've been helpful.

"Yes," replied Alex sheepishly. She paused in thought before adding, "Daddy, what if they know it was me? What if they try to arrest me or something?"

"I don't think that's gonna be the case. Knowing Wren, if he had even a hint of suspicion, he would've been bangin' the door down. I'll be curious if he even brings it up."

"Okay," said Alex, who hesitated before continuing. "What if Jimmy is there? What should I do?"

"We'll watch his expressions and body language," replied Colton. "Remember one of the first rules of negotiation—assess your adversary. If he appears angry, let me deal with it. If his demeanor exudes sadness or fear, speak to him. But under no circumstances, Alex, should you leave with him. We need to be crystal clear on this."

"Yes, Daddy," said Alex. "I should've listened to you and Mom yesterday, but I didn't. Now look."

Colton wiped a few tears from Alex's cheeks. He began to wonder if it was a mistake to bring her today. Colton thought Alex could calm Jimmy down if he appeared at the HPA in a hostile mood. He wanted to avoid a confrontation with the teen.

As they entered the HPA meeting, Colton immediately noticed Wren standing in the middle of the room with his wife and daughters. This was the first meeting attended by Christie and the girls. As Wren was introducing his family to the neighbors, he caught Colton's attention and nodded upward, with a slight smile. Colton's dislike for Wren had become so strong that he wasn't sure if the gesture was a sign of a thaw in their chilled relationship or one of those *aha-I-gotcha-now* looks.

After the exchange of some pleasantries with the attendees, Wren got down to business.

"Ladies and gentlemen, thank you all for coming today," started Wren with his wife and children by his side. "First, let me thank you for making Christie and the girls feel welcome. Circumstances have changed, and I feel better having them with me at all times."

Many of the neighbors mumbled their agreement and looked around the room. Colton noticed the smaller numbers, and he was sure the others did too.

"There is a lot of news to report today, and I'm sorry to say that very little of it is good," continued Wren. Colton heard Alex suck in her breath as she reached for his hand. "The other night, in an unfortunate accident, Gene Andrews was shot. He and his wife did their best to treat the wounds themselves, but infection set in and began to spread through his body. They attempted to walk to the new FEMA facility at 100 Oaks Mall, which, as we all know, was an annex to Vanderbilt Hospital before the collapse of the electric grid. Sadly, I'm told they never made it and Gene died before they got to Hillsboro Pike."

"We'll pray for his wife," said one of the neighbors.

"Very tragic," said another.

"The tragedies continue," interrupted Wren. "Sometime yesterday, Adam Holder was shot and killed in his home." Unconsciously, Colton pulled Alex into his side with his arm around her shielding her from any threats.

People in the room gasped and then the room erupted in conversation. Husbands and wives hugged one another. Mothers brought children closer to them. But Colton immediately looked around the room for Jimmy Holder. He wasn't there.

"What about the boy?" asked one of the neighbors.

"I discovered Adam's body yesterday afternoon," replied Wren. "The back door was open, and there wasn't any sign of a forced entry. Jimmy was missing. Other than Adam's body, there was no other evidence of looting or theft."

One of the female neighbors spoke up from the rear of the room. "Didn't he and Jimmy have a strained relationship? His wife confided in me once about this. Apparently, Jimmy was never comfortable being adopted by Adam."

"I've been told this as well," said another neighbor.

Alex rose on her toes to whisper to Colton, but he knew what she was going to say. It was best to remain passive at this moment and allow the speculation to run its course. These neighbors were developing a narrative that placed the blame for the killing on Jimmy Holder—unwilling, troubled, adopted stepson.

"What's done is done," interrupted Wren. "I felt it was my obligation to look through their home, as we don't have any active law enforcement, much less crime scene investigators. I did find some indication that Jimmy favored his real father, who lives in Antioch. Adam has mentioned to me that their relationship was *troubled.* At this point, there is no reason to speculate further. A couple of us removed Adam's body and buried him in the backyard. The house is locked and secure." Colton gave Alex a squeeze of reassurance, who immediately relaxed against him.

Wren handed his wife a printed flyer, and she gave it to a woman standing near the front. "These flyers have been circulating around the neighborhood. If you haven't seen it, here's the gist. FEMA and the National Guard, per the President's martial law declaration, has begun to enforce compliance on a house-to-house basis. At this time, their efforts are concentrated to our west, where the fires have threatened homes on the other side of Belle Meade Boulevard near Highway 100."

The flyer was passed around the room and the general reaction of most residents was to shake their heads. Colton knew what the declaration provided, and he knew what the President's intentions were—level the playing field to make everyone equally weak, vulnerable, and dependent.

"Are you saying we should comply with this?" asked a neighbor in the front of the room.

"Not necessarily," replied Wren. "That's a personal decision you'll have to make. I just wanted to give everyone a heads-up to be aware of the potential increased military activity in our neighborhood soon. If you have weapons or excess food and supplies, you might want to conceal them from discovery."

A man in the rear of the room challenged Wren. "Shane, with all due respect, how do we know they'll be real military?"

It was a logical question in light of the confrontation the other day between Colton and Wren. Colton decided to help out.

"You'll know because they're more apt to be polite—before they take your food."

"What about this requirement that we evacuate to a FEMA camp?" asked another resident.

"Here's what I've heard," replied Wren. "When they enter your home, they will assess your conditions. If you appear too weak to sustain yourself, then you will immediately be loaded into a military transport and relocated to 100 Oaks or one of the local stadiums or shopping malls in the city."

"Do you mean, like, a football stadium?" asked a woman in attendance with a child. "How would that work?"

"You'll probably sleep in a FEMA tent like after Superstorm Sandy," replied a resident standing next to her.

"You're kidding, right?" replied the young woman.

"Nope. Do you remember all of those refugees at the Superdome in New Orleans after Katrina?" the man asked. "Within forty-eight hours, the Dome was packed with thirty thousand people with no power and not nearly enough supplies to take care of them. The only thing FEMA got right during that fiasco was the massive eighteen-wheeler refrigerated trucks used as makeshift morgues."

The group attending the HPA meeting broke out in conversation among themselves. Colton saw the reality settling in for all of them. They were struggling to survive in their homes, but the thought of becoming a refugee scared them more. Some didn't want to leave their homes only to die in a FEMA camp. Others argued that the government would find a way to take care of them like always.

"Okay, everybody," started Wren. "Once again, this is a decision that you have to make that is best for you and your family. But there is something else I need to bring to your attention that might influence your options."

"What is it?"

"I've had a few of you approach me about a situation taking place just to the north of us at Glen Eden Drive and Hobbs Road," replied Wren. "Apparently, there is a well-organized group of criminals going street to street and looting. They are very methodical, and their procedures leave no doubt about their penchant for ruthlessness. It is a potentially dangerous situation for all of us if they are moving this way."

Once again, more murmurs flared up between the neighbors. Colton heard one man exclaim, "I'm outta here," as he left the building. Most of the residents questioned why the National Guard didn't do something.

Wren continued. "I need a couple of you folks who live on the north end of the neighborhood to scout their activities and report back to me at my home as soon as possible. We need to ascertain their intentions. If they are moving in an organized fashion toward us, we'll face a dangerous situation very soon."

Wren finished up the meeting by recruiting his scouts and saying goodbye to a few residents who said they were going to the FEMA camps after hearing today's update. Colton took Alex by the hand and began to lead her out of the HPA house when he heard Wren's voice.

"Mr. Ryman, may I speak with you before you leave?" asked Wren.

Mr. Ryman? Oh boy, here we go.

CHAPTER 29

DAY TEN
4:00 p.m., September 18
Ryman Residence
Nashville, Tennessee

"I don't trust him," said Madison forcefully as Colton tried to explain Wren's attempt at extending the proverbial olive branch. Following the HPA meeting earlier, Wren apologized for getting off on the wrong foot with Colton and his entire family. He even used his wife and children to warm up to Alex. Alex responded favorably to the gesture and was unaware of the obvious ploy employed by Wren to soften the tensions between the two families. However, on the walk home from the HPA meeting, Alex's spirits were lifted considerably. *That was a good thing.*

"Maddie, I agree that we have to take baby steps with him," said Colton. "But, I genuinely believe he's scared. I'm sure he knows why Andrews was shot. He probably also knows Holder was with Andrews that night." Colton took a long drink of water before continuing.

"Holder's death is another matter. I'm sure he blames Jimmy, although he might believe I'm involved with his death after our confrontation at the HPA meeting the other day. He may be afraid of me. Who knows? Regardless, his sidekicks who gave him strength are gone now."

"But why you?" asked Madison, exhibiting some fear in her voice, which explained her hostile attitude toward the proposed unholy alliance with Wren. Notwithstanding the fact that the Ryman family was directly responsible for the deaths of Wren's collaborators, joining the HPA leadership team seemed to be a death wish.

"Why not me?" asked Colton. "Why not keep our friends close, but our enemies closer. Also, we are facing a number of threats to our neighborhood now. Despite the rain, as you can tell by the smell of smoke, the fires are still burning to our west. As the winds pick up, they'll continue to head our way."

The Rymans, sitting on the front steps together, were momentarily distracted by a group of people walking in the middle of the street. Pushing everything from baby strollers to shopping carts, the people appeared lethargic and disoriented. The refugees, who seemed to be headed for 100 Oaks, didn't make the effort to look in the Rymans' direction.

After seventy-two hours, the human body entered into a phase in which it started to break down protein in muscles. The brain needed energy to function, so it sought out glucose from the body. The muscles broke down further in order to feed the brain. This process began to accelerate, zapping the average human being of energy and weakening their immune systems.

After seven to ten days without food, the average person would become virtually incapacitated. While some studies have shown the body might survive up to twenty-one days without sustenance, that period was lessened considerably due to dehydration. In third world nations, where electricity and nutritional supplements were scarce, the number one cause of death was a protein-energy malnutrition characterized by edema, a distended belly, and irritability.

Colton continued. "The military is stepping up its efforts to confiscate supplies and weapons. They'll be banging on our front door soon. Compare the way we look to those folks down on the street. Our clothes are clean and we appear to be well fed. If we have to open up our cupboards and pretend we're starvin', they ain't gonna buy it."

"So what are we supposed to do, starve ourselves?" asked Madison.

"No, but we need to rough up our appearance a little bit," replied Colton. "I'm afraid we're standing out too much."

"Fine, but what does this have to do with Wren?" asked Madison.

"Nothing, exactly, but just our overall situation," replied Colton. "We're threatened by the fires and the National Guard. Now there's this new gang of looters to the north, who are systematically moving through the neighborhood towards us."

Madison squirmed on the hard brick pavers. The subject matter also made her uncomfortable. Colton didn't want to scare his wife, but she needed to understand why he felt compelled to join forces with Wren and the neighbors.

Initially, Colton felt a lone-wolf strategy was the best approach to surviving. They had more food and supplies than others. The bulk of the unrest was still in the city, although it was now getting closer based on the increasing number of residents opting for the nearby FEMA camps.

However, the wheels seemed to be falling off the wagon of their community, and the go-it-alone approach might lead to a certain death. Banding together with the neighbors to ward off their most imminent threat from the north might ensure their survival.

"How close are they?" asked Madison.

"Only about a mile, but they seem to be taking their time moving our way," replied Colton. "Wren sent some scouts out today to watch their activities. He'll get a report back and discuss it with me tomorrow."

Madison remained quiet for a moment. Alex hadn't said a word during the entire conversation. Colton couldn't determine if they were digesting his words or if their attitudes were shifting. He had to provide his family a steady mix of reality and optimism. Poor mental health, whether through malnutrition or loss of hope, would lead to their downfall. It was critical that they all keep a positive state of mind.

First of all, it was essential to situational readiness. A distracted mind made you vulnerable to surprise. A poor state of mind could result in letting down your guard and, therefore, exposing yourself to attack. In this dystopian world, they had to constantly be prepared to defend themselves against potential threats. Colton had to keep the girls in this survival mind-set without breaking their spirit.

Secondly, depression and suicide could be contagious if Colton didn't address it before it set in. Alex's killing of Holder was only one aspect of the dark cloud of depression he was trying to ward off. Madison was becoming increasingly quiet and withdrawn. Colton was concerned she was having difficulty overcoming her anxiety and fear. Colton's solution was to provide his wife common ground with others situated like them, to give and receive support.

Colton wasn't naïve. He'd watched Wren and the other regular attendees of the HPA carefully. As the circle of neighbors grew smaller, his vision of the entire situation became clearer. There was strength in loyalty, not necessarily in numbers. He'd have to determine where the residents' loyalties lay.

"I say we go for it, Mom," said Alex, breaking her silence. "I've noticed how the people look up to Daddy now. After you showed them the video, their attitudes changed."

"Yeah, I guess that did calm down the witch hunt," said Madison.

"Also, don't forget," continued Alex. "Daddy really put Wren in his place. There was a huge difference between today's meeting and the one just two days ago. I know I'd feel better if we could count on others too."

"So is that a yes vote for working with the HPA?" asked Colton.

"Yes," replied Alex.

"Maddie, what say you?" asked Colton.

Madison pondered for a moment and then smiled. "I vote a reluctant yes," she said finally. "At first, let's use them to repel the bad guys. After that, we should reevaluate. I don't want the neighbors thinking they can come over for supper."

"Fair enough," agreed Colton.

Now that the issue of working with Wren and the HPA to repel the threat was agreed upon, Colton knew he'd have to address the bigger question at some point—*should we stay, or should we go?*

CHAPTER 30

DAY ELEVEN
Noon, September 19
HPA Meeting House
Trimble Rd. & Lynnwood Blvd.
Belle Meade, Tennessee

Colton listened to the reports from the scouts Wren sent out yesterday and he began to question the wisdom of taking on the gang of thugs that called themselves COBRA. The COBRA gang traveled in one big pack, with a show of overwhelming force. After they pulled onto a street in their dilapidated but operating sixties model cars and trucks, the leader brought the convoy to a halt. They honked their horns for a minute or two to get the attention of the residents. Then their leader emerged with a bullhorn.

After hearing the details, Colton and Wren agreed they needed to hurry up the meeting and see these guys in action for themselves. But based upon COBRA's daily progress, they needed to be stopped immediately. After today, COBRA would be working their way down Sunnybrook Drive, only two blocks to their north.

"I won't gloss over the facts to make you feel better," started Colton, addressing the HPA residents for the first time. There were nearly twenty men and eleven women in attendance. "The residents to our north are fleeing their homes in the wake of this group's advance towards us. Many are opting for 100 Oaks. Others are walking to the south and more rural areas such as Williamson County. We have learned that this group, which calls themselves COBRA, has taken up residency in Harpeth Hall and are spreading their reign of terror outward from there."

Harpeth Hall was an all-girls school with an excellent reputation built up over one hundred and fifty years. Only a few miles away from the Ryman home, Colton and Madison had debated whether to enroll Alex there when she was old enough to enter fifth grade.

They chose Davidson Academy even though it was much farther away because it was co-ed. They agreed Alex could get a more well-rounded life experience attending a school with boys. Granted, that opened Alex up for the usual hazing such as bra snaps or insults. Madison argued the time for Alex to experience the hatefulness of others was not when she was entering the grown-up world for the first time.

Colton continued. "The houses on Belle Meade Boulevard have the protection of law enforcement and the National Guardsmen. I suppose status does gain you privileges after the world as we know it comes to an end. But don't envy them too much. The fires continue to burn out of control and are now on this side of Highway 100."

"Can we contact them somehow and gain their assistance?" asked one of the neighbors.

"We tried that yesterday, and the response was simple—*we have our orders*," interjected Wren. "I'm afraid we'll have to fight for ourselves."

One man put his hand in the air before he began to speak. "How many are there?"

"Our scouts estimate that the gang is made-up of eighteen to twenty well-armed men," replied Wren.

"Are those military guys gonna help us?" asked one resident, referring to the phony National Guardsmen who attended one of the early meetings. Colton let Wren answer that one.

"Um, no. They've moved on. I mean, they were recalled to their unit."

"How are we supposed to fight twenty looters on our own?" asked another neighbor. "We're not soldiers."

Colton took this one, which gave him an opportunity to instill confidence in the group. "How do we stop that? We have to create a larger force. Everybody must fight. You need to go home and explain to your neighbors who didn't come today to be ready. We have the element of surprise on our side. We know the neighborhood and they don't."

"I don't have a gun."

"Me either."

"I only have a twenty-two. It'll barely take down a squirrel."

Wren stepped in. "We'll have weapons for everyone. Maybe even two—a rifle and a handgun. Ammo too. We'll meet here at dawn at which time I can assure you, everybody will be well armed."

The group began to speak among themselves. The conversations surrounding the use of weapons used to take place at wine and cheese parties or during political fund-raisers. Now the gun debate was couched in reality.

"Everyone, listen up," started Colton. "We'll take the battle to them. Today, we're going to watch their methods. We'll find a flaw and catch them off guard. We have to take a stand now, or they will overrun us in a matter of days."

From the heads nodding in the crowd and the slaps on the backs of one another, it appeared Colton was garnering a consensus. These folks needed to support one another because there was a good chance several wouldn't make it home.

"I want all of you to go home and spend time with your families. Kiss the ones you love and make peace with God. Be here at dawn tomorrow and bring your neighbors."

The attendees began to file out of the HPA meeting house, leaving Wren and two men who Colton recognized but had never formally met.

"Colton, I want you to meet Wilson Holt and his neighbor Sammy Shepherd," started Wren. "They both live up on Sunnybrook Drive." The men exchanged handshakes.

"By our calculations, our homes will be the first ones on the hit list," said Shepherd. "From what we've observed the last couple of days, there won't be anything left unless we take a stand."

Colton suggested they take a walk up the street and then sneak through the backyards. He wanted to observe the methods used by this COBRA gang. As they walked, Shepherd and Holt related their observations and analysis to Colton and Wren.

COBRA usually traveled by two *land yachts*, as Colton used to call them. A land yacht from the sixties was a big four-door Cadillac or Lincoln. Built in the days before gas mileage was an issue, six men could fit inside of them with relative ease.

Their third vehicle was a military surplus M35 cargo truck, commonly referred to as a Deuce and a Half. In addition to functioning as a troop carrier, it was ideal for use by COBRA as a loot carrier.

They usually started their activities in the afternoon. Apparently, they were undisciplined and partied late into the night following the day's raids. Holt pointed out that on two occasions, men stood up to the thugs in an attempt to deny access to their homes or their wives. This didn't end well either time. The COBRA thugs pummeled the men mercilessly and kidnapped the women.

These vicious marauders preferred to beat their victims, which was a much more personal method of murder. Thus far, according to Shepherd and Holt, gunshots hadn't been heard. Colton surmised there was more to this group than met the eye.

Holt led the contingent northward on Lynnwood Boulevard to where COBRA was in the process of a raid. As the HPA group cautiously approached the homes on Signal Hill Drive, several of the thugs were in the midst of beating a man and his son to death in the front yard of their home.

Colton was about to learn for himself what embodied the depravity of man.

CHAPTER 31

DAY ELEVEN
4:00 p.m., September 19
Ryman Residence
Belle Meade, Tennessee

Madison presented Colton with her updated inventory, a projected meal plan, and some calculations based on maintaining their current food levels. Colton studied the Farm Bureau insurance calendar used by Madison to plan out their meals. He'd better grow fond of beans and rice.

"Well, at least we have a date," started Colton. "It's better to know when we'll run out than speculate and get caught off guard. To extend our food supply, we have to procure more from our neighbors or the power has to come on in a hurry. Even then, there's no guarantee the trucks will begin running and delivering food to the grocery stores."

"If the power remains out much longer, we'll have to make a decision about staying here," added Madison. Colton was glad to hear her think in these terms. He didn't want to leave either. Colton loved their home so much he was willing to risk his life against a band of marauders, a decision he'd second-guessed repeatedly in the last few hours.

"I wish there was a farmers' market around," said Colton. "I could trade them something we don't need for food or even seeds. If we can make it through the winter, we could plant our garden."

Madison took the calendar back and started counting days with the tip of a pencil until she reached the third week of October. "Growing up in the mid-state, I remember most crops were harvested in September and October. If there is any hope of supplementing our food supply with fresh vegetables, it would have to occur in the next four weeks. That's assuming, of course, we could find a farmer willing to trade with us."

"My biggest fear about traveling into the countryside is that once we leave that garage, everybody and their brother will know about the Wagoneer," said Colton. "It's a miracle we've kept it hidden this long. If I travel out of the county, there is no guarantee I can get back in one piece."

"I agree. We've got to save the Wagoneer as our last method of escape."

Colton walked across the living room and peered through the makeshift peepholes he'd created to monitor the outside. When he returned to the kitchen, he asked Madison how long Alex had been sleeping. They'd switched up their routine so that Alex could take the night shift and Colton could get a good night's sleep.

"She's been sleeping four hours," replied Madison as she handed him an MRE bar. She was diligent about feeding the family in five or six small meals a day to maintain their energy levels.

"When Alex wakes up, we'll make a trip over to the O'Malleys'," started Colton. "I found it odd that they didn't have any vegetable seeds stored. I must have overlooked them. In the coming weeks, their garden is going to provide a few things like carrots, potatoes, and squash."

"That will help," added Madison somewhat enthusiastically.

"Maddie, have you thought more about leaving?" asked Colton.

"To where?"

"I don't know. I mean, I have an idea that I've been bouncing around in my head."

Madison had been thinking about the issue, and she began to share all of the variables with Colton. "Here's the way I see it," she started. "Of course, I'd like to hunker down with our supplies and ride out the storm until the world gets back on its feet. But we don't know when that will be."

"Do you get the sense the walls are closing in on us?" asked

Colton, unafraid now to broach the subject with his wife.

"I do. The fires might get under control with a couple solid days of rain, but the National Guard won't stop their house-to-house searches until they take everything we have. Even if we fool them the first time, when they drive by in a week or two and see that we're still here, they'll try again."

"That's true," said Colton.

"Then there's tomorrow," said Madison, waving the calender in the air. "My husband, top-notch talent agent, is going to war with a bunch of COBRAs. You're not an ex-Marine or some fictional guy who can all of a sudden charge headlong into the teeth of the enemy, mowing them down with your new machine gun over there without breaking a sweat." Madison nodded to the AR-15 slung over the back of the kitchen chair.

"I don't have to do this, you know," said Colton. "We can pack up now and leave. I'd imagined staying here until the recovery effort kicks in, but I don't see it happenin', do you?"

"Nope, which is why I did this today," replied Madison. "Can we survive here until the power is restored? Even if you're successful in repelling these guys tomorrow, there will be another group right behind them eventually. Is that the way we want to live?"

Colton was relieved to have this conversation. He was not anxious to leave, but now he knew he wouldn't have to convince Madison to leave their home.

"I feel better about headin' out to the country now than I did a week ago," said Colton. "The threats we face are a big factor. We can only live under this type of pressure for so long. I don't know what we'll face away from Nashville, but there will be less of them."

Madison reached out and held his hand, which gave him the strength to continue.

"The survival of our family rests on our shoulders, and if we find ourselves in an environment that isn't conducive to safety, we need to make a choice. We either leave an environment that is toxic, or we stand firm and defend it. Before that choice is made, we need to weigh our options carefully, including the risks and the odds of surviving these threats. Really, what it all comes down to is which scenario gives us the best opportunity to survive and then create a new life for ourselves where we can thrive."

"Colt, I've always trusted your judgment," said Madison. "Throughout our lives together, you've always been a loving husband and a great father to Alex. Whatever you decide, I'm with ya, Mr. Ryman."

"I love you, and our daughter is our life," started Colton. "I don't care where we live as long as we're together."

Madison rose from her seat and kissed Colton. During the last two weeks, the two hadn't shared many tender moments together. It felt good.

"Hey," interrupted a sleepy-eyed Alex. "You two need to get a room."

Madison and Colton laughed as he replied, "Indeed we do!"

CHAPTER 32

DAY TWELVE
Predawn, September 20
HPA Meeting House
Trimble Rd. & Lynnwood Blvd.
Belle Meade, Tennessee

Colton decided it was a risk worth taking. He'd debated the point as he got ready this morning and ultimately decided to carry the Camp Chef cooktop system, the propane, and coffee fixin's in Mrs. Abercrombie's wheelbarrow. The gesture was designed to lift the morale and spirits of the neighbors who were going to risk their lives to protect their families and homes. He no longer concerned himself with disclosing his ownership of these valuable items. You had to live to enjoy life.

Madison didn't cry when he left this morning. She gave him the support and love he needed to face an evil he knew existed but never imagined he'd have to confront. Undoubtedly, she and Alex would be hand-wringing to an extent. His girls didn't need this additional stress. Nobody did. However, it was the world they lived in now.

While Colton brewed the coffee, Wren quickly organized and displayed the entire arsenal retrieved from Holder's basement. Firearms were separated by handguns, rifles, and shotguns. Ammunition was neatly stacked next to its corresponding weapon. Naturally, Colton did not disclose his acquisition of the two AR-15 rifles. Colton had brought the Taurus nine millimeter in his paddle holster and intended to pick out another weapon to compliment it.

"Colton," started Wren, "I'd like you to meet Danielle Faber. Danielle's recently completed the National Rifle Association's

Certified Coach Program. She's going to give our people a crash course in firearms training."

"Good morning," said Colton, extending his hand to the woman, who was dressed in black jeans and a loosely fitting black shirt. He wondered if she led a double life as a ninja.

"My pleasure, Colton," she replied. "Before the others arrive, why don't we select weapons for you and Shane first. Have you trained with firearms before?"

"No," replied Colton. "What does a certified coach do?"

"I began in a part-time position at the Nashville Gun Club years ago and had been promoted to a full-time instructor in the five stand competition."

"What's that?"

"Five stand is a cross between skeet, trap, and clay targeting. It's the closest thing there is to a video game in sporting gun competitions. Targets are flying in all directions, at various speeds, and in unpredictable combinations."

"Sounds like you need great reflexes and concentration for that," said Colton.

"Exactly," started Faber. "It's not unlike what we might experience today."

"We?"

"Of course," replied Faber. "I wouldn't miss this for the world. Now, let's pick a weapon for you. I see you have a nine-millimeter Taurus tucked away there. Do you have spare magazines?"

"No."

Faber walked toward the end of the tables arranged in the Brileys' living room and fumbled through a pile of empty magazines. She reached out her hand to Colton.

"May I?"

Colton pulled the gun out and handed it to her. Within seconds, she'd dropped the magazine and racked the slide to clear the weapon. It was effortless.

Several residents began to arrive and helped themselves to the coffee. Colton noticed the difference in their attitudes immediately. A simple gesture of kindness lifted their spirits. The room began to fill with chatter.

"I found three more mags for you," said Faber. "Also, here are a hundred rounds of nine millimeter. I have an idea for your complimentary weapon."

Colton followed her down the row of tables as a crowd began to gather around. She led him to a rifle that was not that much different in design from the AR-15s.

"The gentlemen who owned this collection had good taste in weaponry," started Faber. "Not everyone has one of these." She handed the folded-up rifle to Colton.

"It seems compact."

"It folds up to a tight sixteen inches for easy storage," said Faber. "The barrel unfolds and snaps in place, and the stock is adjustable for your particular use and comfort. Go ahead, get her ready."

Colton snapped everything into place and loved the slim, lightweight feel of the four-pound carbine. She handed him three more magazines.

"This is the Kel-Tec Sub 2000 chambered in nine millimeter," said Faber. "Both of your weapons use the same round, which will help you in a battle situation. Get your spare magazines loaded while I get these other guys outfitted."

"Thank you," said Colton. He was impressed with her knowledge and straightforward approach to gun selection. He was anxious to go through her crash course on gun handling.

It was after 7:00 a.m. when the entire HPA contingent had arrived and was assigned weapons. Colton counted twenty-one men and two women, plus himself. In addition to Faber, Gene Andrew's wife, Kayla, was present. This concerned Colton somewhat. If she knew of Gene's whereabouts the night he was shot, then she would blame Colton for her husband's death. Colton made a mental note to watch out for friendly fire.

"Okay, everyone, let's get started," said Faber. "Gather around. First, by a show of hands, how many of you have been through an NRA firearms training course?"

No one.

"Well, let me ask this. How many of you have used a firearm before?"

Three hands were raised, but Colton abstained.

Just wonderful.

"Then we've got some work to do." Faber laughed. Colton was glad she thought it was funny. He was pleased that all of the HPA army seemed to be focused and intent on learning. He needed this training as well.

Faber started the ten-minute course. "First, always point the gun in a safe direction. This is the primary rule of gun safety. If your weapon is drawn and ready, keep it pointed at the ground in front of you. Just remember, common sense will dictate the safest direction based on the circumstances.

"Second, always keep your finger off the trigger until you're ready to fire the weapon. Hold your index finger straight out like this. And rest it on the trigger guard. Again, very important, do not touch the trigger until you are ready to fire.

"Third, be absolutely sure you've identified your target beyond any doubt. Also, be aware of everything that is downrange of your target, which includes your friends. Depending upon the circumstances today, you may catch your adversaries in a cross fire. This will give you the upper hand, but it could also be dangerous. Always think first, shoot second.

"Fourth, the proper stance should have your feet shoulder-width apart, like this, with your left foot forward, if you're right-handed. The opposite applies if your left hand is dominant. Don't lock your knees and make sure you are properly balanced. Let me summarize. Two hands, feet shoulder-width, one foot forward, knees bent, seek balance.

"Fifth, once the decision to shoot is made, obtain your target in your sights and steady the gun with your other hand. Make sure the gun is level by aligning the top of the rear sight with the top of the front post. Some of you have optics on your rifles, so your job will be much easier.

"Okay, last step. It's time to shoot. Control your breathing and relax. This will be hard for all of you to do in the midst of a confrontation. Gently squeeze the trigger and the gun will fire. Some of you will experience more recoil than others, so be sure to reacquire your target before you shoot again. The tendency will be to empty your magazine, hoping for the best. You're not trained in switching magazines and your ammo levels are low. You need to discipline yourself and strive for quality, not quantity. Above all, breathe and relax throughout the process."

Faber replaced her sidearm in a shoulder holster and slung the AR-15 over her shoulder. She nodded to Colton, indicating she was finished. Colton knew this group should have practiced together like he'd done with Madison and Alex. Even the dry-fire practice sessions would've helped, but there wasn't time. They needed to get in position and discuss strategy. But first, he needed to get them mentally ready. Like Faber, Colton slung his new rifle over his shoulder.

"In a perfect world, we'd have attended an NRA class and learned these basic firearm rules without the pressure of what we're going to face later. Today, you'll learn there are no training courses to teach you how to take another man's life. Just remember. Self-defense is not just the point where murder ends and defense of your life begins. It's also a state of mind that begins with the belief that your life is worth defending."

The nearly two dozen faces stared back at Colton and nodded. They were scared, just like he was. But the looks of determination told Colton they were ready to survive.

CHAPTER 33

DAY TWELVE
Noon, September 20
Sunnybrook Drive
Belle Meade, Tennessee

Colton broke up the two dozen members of the HPA squad into twelve groups of two. He paired himself with Wren. Faber was paired with Mrs. Andrews. Hopefully, she would prevent Mrs. Andrews from shooting Colton in the back.

The COBRA gang was unpredictable. Because of their proximity to the neighborhood and their consistent southern trajectory, the ability to observe their routine was not available. Colton had to space the twelve teams according to his prediction of their next move, with the help of a *suggested route.*

Sunnybrook Drive was the next logical stop for the COBRA marauders. Their other option was to come directly down Lynnwood, which would've put them at the front door of the HPA meeting house—with the next stop, Harding Place.

Colton intended to steer the thugs east onto Sunnybrook. There were only a few homes on a fairly short stretch before the road took a sharp right turn toward the south. Faber took three teams to the north side of Sunnybrook to alert the residents to remain in their homes or wait at the HPA meeting house until the conclusion—whatever that looked like.

Two teams were then sent to the Lynnwood intersection and just below the ninety-degree turn on Sunnybrook. Their jobs were simple. Block the road with any vehicle available. The four members of these teams were able to place cars into neutral and roll them into the middle of the street to resemble an accident or that they'd stalled. Doors were left open, and hoods were raised, leaving the illusion that this was a natural result of the solar flare rather than something staged. To add effect, the teams siphoned antifreeze onto the street. The goal was to force the COBRA vehicles onto Sunnybrook, where they would be surrounded by the HPA neighbors.

Everyone went about their business diligently. Colton positioned himself in the center of activity. Most of the homes were vacant, and a few residents left for the safety of the HPA meeting house. One couple on the south side of Sunnybrook was armed and joined the fight.

The homes on Sunnybrook were set back from the road roughly two hundred feet or more. All of the lawns were cleared except for a few dozen mature oaks. There was little cover for the HPA to use when the moment for action came. They would have to hide around the homes and then use the cover of the massive oak tree trunks to advance toward the road. The whole setup was conducive to the neighbors firing wildly without discipline.

The alternative was not much better. If the COBRA thugs concentrated their efforts on one home at a time, which was their apparent method of operation, the two-man team assigned to that home would be easily overrun. By necessity, COBRA would have to be engaged out in the open. They wouldn't be able to use their vehicles for protective cover—the cross fire Colton created would take care of that. The lack of experienced shooters, including himself, was the HPA's greatest weakness.

Many of these details, and the unforeseen scenarios, had run through Colton's mind as he tossed and turned last night, getting very little sleep. But the one important issue left unresolved was who would take the first shot. In Colton's mind, COBRA was the aggressor. They'd proven themselves to be nothing but a loosely organized group of criminals and thugs with a heinous agenda—steal and kill.

He'd prayed about it with Madison. He asked God to give him the strength to take another man's life—for the second time. The unresolved issue for Colton was whether taking the first shot today was self-defense or murder. Early this morning, he surmised he'd know when the time came. The sound of the big diesel engine in the M35 signaled the time was now.

Colton and Wren crouched behind a block and brick wall surrounding the front porch of a ranch-style house, which was slightly elevated above the street. The wall gave Colton some cover and the peace of mind that he would be protected from return fire if it came to that. As the M35 came to a stop in front of his location, he instantly became aware that he would experience more return fire than that night in his backyard.

As the motor of the big military truck was shut off, the engines of the trailing Cadillac and Buick followed suit. At least two dozen men jumped out of the vehicles, dressed in black cargo pants and tight black tee shirts. Some wore berets and a few wore green, black, and red-striped armbands. Their dark sunglasses and rifles completed a menacing, fear-inspiring look. If their intention was to frighten people into submission, then mission accomplished. Except, not today, thought Colton.

A large man rose up from the back of the truck bed. His bald head stood out among the others, who all wore some type of hat. He was wearing a tactical vest that included a sidearm. A bandolier of shotgun shells crossed his chest. Colton immediately conjured up an image of a Somalian warlord from the *Captain Phillips* movie. Except this man was far more threatening.

He lifted a megaphone and began to speak into it.

"My name is Viper Rex, and these gentlemen are members of COBRA." The men dispersed around the vehicles all nodded their heads.

"We are not here to cause you any harm. We come in peace!"

All of the men started to laugh and raised their weapons into the air.

"My message is a simple one. Do not resist, or you will die. This is our time now. You owe us!" As if on cue, the men raised their weapons and began to scan the trees and homes with their sights.

Colton immediately looked to make sure his people were well hidden. Either they were, or they'd run off. He hoped it was the former.

"You will have five minutes to leave your homes and stand in the middle of the street. You will not be harmed unless you resist." Colton knew he was lying based upon his observations from yesterday. Only the naïve would believe a criminal like this.

Colton leaned over to Wren and whispered, "You're a political scientist, what does he mean by *you owe us*?"

"COBRA is the acronym for the Coalition of Blacks for Reparations in America. It was founded about the time the New Black Panther Party was organized in the eighties. Outwardly, the two organizations claim there is no legal relationship, but they appear to be part of a black nationalist movement seeking reparations for African descendants residing in the United States."

"Reparations for what?" asked Colton as he kept an eye on Viper Rex.

"Slavery," replied Wren.

The megaphone came to life with a blare of its horn. "Time's up, white people. We are here for an apology that is long overdue. If you are unwilling to face us and issue a proper apology, then we will seek atonement from you. Today, we will take a small step toward squaring things for our African brothers!"

Some of the men began shouting and now, for added terroristic effect, included firing their weapons into the air. Wren and Colton immediately ducked behind the protective wall. Colton was frightened, but they had no choice. They had to fight.

These people were no different from ideological terrorists like ISIS or the KKK. They were inherently racist and were using the horrific acts of slavery from one hundred fifty years ago to justify their criminal activities of today.

Colton had always wondered why this country couldn't become color blind. Why must things be couched in terms of race? *First black this. Only white that.* He'd hoped this catastrophic event might reset that attitude in America. Obviously, he was wrong. Perhaps it was human nature for humans to default into their comfort zones and seek out like-minded individuals in a time of crisis. He doubted that was the case with Viper Rex and his gang of thugs. They were nothing but killers and thieves looking to take advantage of people's weakened state courtesy of a solar flare.

Without giving it further thought, Colton rose up over the wall, fired, and immediately killed his first COBRA. His blood was red, just like Colton's.

CHAPTER 34

DAY TWELVE
Noon, September 20
Sunnybrook Drive
Belle Meade, Tennessee

Faber knew that, unlike the movies, people didn't stand out in the open and calmly fire at their enemy. When a person was being shot at, his primary concern was not to die. This was a basic survival instinct held by all human beings who were not suicidal maniacs. It took a real fool or tough guy to ignore bullets flying around their body while trying to return fire.

In the case of COBRA, there were no other options but to stand and fight. Sometimes, a hero was a coward that had been driven into a corner. COBRA was surrounded. To their credit, it took a great deal of bravery not to cower under their vehicles and beg for mercy. To their detriment, it was foolish to rely solely on the bravado of Viper Rex and not contemplate that someone might fight back at some point.

Bullets flew in all directions, mostly missing their mark. Going to the range and shooting a firearm in a non-stressed, relaxed atmosphere was far different than an engaged firefight. At the range, you had plenty of time to aim at the target, with a normal heart rate, relaxed mind, and ample time to steady your weapon.

Faber quickly realized that this uncontrolled environment elevated her heart rate, and stress hormones pumped adrenaline through her body in a way she'd never experienced before. Unlike the others assisting her, she'd trained using heart rate variability. At her best, she was only twenty percent accurate—within twenty feet! From her position crouched behind a stalled car, she was nearly two hundred feet from her target.

She tried to steady her nerves despite the distraction of Mrs. Andrews's crying. Faber understood the need for the widow to lash out following the death of her husband, but this was not the time. To avoid an unfortunate accident, Faber relieved Mrs. Andrews of her handgun for everyone's protection, including her own. Faber didn't want to get shot by the distraught woman.

The last vehicle in the caravan started up, and the men jumped in as it pulled away. Immediately, Faber became comfortable with the new target—the Buick's tires. Using her scoped Remington 700 target rifle, she fired two rounds and flattened the left-side tires.

From her right, the explosion of a shotgun rang out, killing the driver. The remaining men inside the vehicle returned fire, but they simply shredded the oak trees. They were trapped, and the neighbors at the Lynnwood intersection began to close in, indiscriminately firing into the Buick. After a steady barrage of gunfire, the occupants of the Buick were dead.

To her left, more volleys pelted the brick façade of the house next door. A scream could be heard, and then she saw the body of one of the residents roll down the concrete steps onto the driveway. An arm shot up above a hedgerow and fired into the air, striking the oak trees thirty feet in front of them. The scene resembled a firefight in the streets of Syria aired on the nightly news—gunmen using the *stick the weapon around the corner and let her rip* technique. It was a waste of ammo. And it gave away the shooter's position. The hedgerow was no match for the return fire from one of the COBRAs' AK-47s. At least thirty rounds peppered the boxwoods, instantly killing the man behind them.

Suddenly, the M35 roared to life and lurched forward. Bullets pelted the steel frame, but it continued. Faber fired three shots in an attempt to take out the tires, but missed her mark. Across the street, she saw Ryman and Wren give chase. Wren maneuvered his way through the trees toward the remaining car, which was stalled in the road.

Sunnybrook Drive was littered with bodies, but the M35 was making an escape with a driver and four men, who continued to pour rounds into the trees on both sides of Sunnybrook.

Across the street, Ryman worked his way through the trees, dodging gunfire that embedded into the trunks. Faber decided to join the fray. They were trying to escape and appeared to be headed for the back side of Harpeth Hall. She had to keep them in the kill zone. More importantly, she couldn't see the leader—Viper Rex. *He can't get away!*

CHAPTER 35

DAY TWELVE
Early Afternoon, September 20
Sunnybrook Drive
Belle Meade, Tennessee

When Colton heard the big diesel engine fire up, he knew the M35 and Viper Rex were trying to escape. Colton inserted a full magazine into his Sub 2000 and instructed Wren to do the same with his handgun. Wren would make sure the stalled Caddy was secure and its pinned-down occupants were dealt with while Colton chased the head of the snake—Viper Rex.

To avoid being shot, a person dodged, took cover, and hid from the attacker. At the same time, a moving person was a difficult target to hit and was a terrible shot when returning fire. When taking cover, the idea was to remain behind something solid that would stop incoming bullets. Despite finding concealment, a person was still vulnerable to enemy fire, but decreased the chance of getting shot.

Colton made his way to the protective cover of an oak tree while Wren distracted the remaining COBRA marauders with several rounds of suppressive fire. Then it was Colton's turn to open fire on the attackers. When they ducked for cover, Colton shouted, "Move," indicating it was safe for Wren to break his cover position and run behind a tree. It was important for each man to maintain his suppressive fire while the other was on the move.

The two alternated this tactic as Colton raced toward the east in chase of Viper Rex and Wren moved to finish off the remaining two gunmen in the Cadillac.

A loud screech came from the area where the M35 turned down a narrow drive near the back of the Harpeth Hall complex. Curse words were emitted in all directions as the M35, overly broad for the driveway, got stuck between two trees. The driver and the passenger were wedged in.

Three gunmen jumped from the back of the truck and opened fire on the six members of the HPA to Colton's right. Viper Rex hoisted himself over the left side and, after looking in all directions, began running through the side yard of the home toward the rear of Harpeth Hall.

Colton noticed Viper Rex was limping. He was wounded. With the COBRA men preoccupied to the right, Colton sprinted across the street in pursuit of his prey.

A shot rang out from his immediate left, startling Colton, which caused him to stumble and fall to the ground, bloodying both elbows. The driver's side window of the truck shattered, and blood exploded on the inside of the windshield. Colton looked over and saw Faber reload her rifle. She joined his side.

"You okay, cowboy?" asked Faber, who kneeled down and kept her rifle ready. "There's easier ways to take cover, you know."

"Yeah, thanks," said Colton as he dusted himself off. He instinctively ducked as bullets shattered the rear window of the M35's cab, killing the passenger. "Should we go after him?"

"There are lots of things to consider," started Faber, speaking louder as gunfire continued a hundred feet to their rear. "Does he have reinforcements? Do you know anything about the layout of the campus or the insides of the buildings?"

"I know enough to know this," replied Colton, "if we don't take him out, he'll be back with a vengeance."

"We could be running into the viper's nest."

"A wounded one, however. He was limping when he ran through the yards."

"Lead the way, boss!" said Faber.

Colton had toured the Harpeth Hall campus six years ago when they were making a decision about Alex's school. Naturally, the tour consisted of the most well-known buildings like Souby Hall, the

Carell Library, and the Patton Visual Arts Center.

"This is just a hunch, but let's try the gymnasium first," started Colton. The two jogged through the trees until they found the parking lot for the Alumni Relations building. "The gym would have locker rooms, medical facilities, and food concessions."

"I'll watch our backs. Let's go."

"Follow me. We'll take this path here to the rear of the gym."

The two methodically made their way down a sidewalk through the woods. Viper Rex could be armed and waiting for them behind the thick underbrush or one of the hundred-year-old oaks. Colton walked heel to toe in an attempt to conceal the sound of his feet on the paved walkway.

The sounds of gunfire on the other side of the woods began to dissipate, which allowed Colton to hear the sound of a door closing up ahead. He stopped and immediately dropped to one knee, wincing from the earlier scrape.

"The rear door to the gym just closed. If he suspects we've trailed him, he'll be waiting for us. Are you sure you wanna do this?"

"What if I say no?" asked Faber.

"I'm goin' in without you," replied Colton boldly.

"Let's not waste any time. Go!"

Colton raced across the loading dock area and made his way to the rear fire exit. He gave Faber another look and nodded. She drew her sidearm and nodded back.

"Blood," said Colton, pointing at the ground.

Colton flung open the door, and the two entered the dark hallway in a low crouch. Colton helped the door close slowly. If the light spreading down the hallway didn't draw attention, he didn't want the slamming door to give away their presence.

Faber found Colton and whispered, "Stop and close your eyes for a moment. Then open them briefly and close them again. This will help your eyes adjust to the darkness."

They heard a crash coming from within the gym. Suddenly, a lantern illuminated the space. Colton and Faber pressed their backs against the wall and listened. Someone was groaning. Then the ripping sound of an adhesive tape being unwound could be heard.

Colton whispered, "He's been shot. Probably the leg. Follow me."

They inched along the wall until they reached the opening to the gym. To their left and right were temporary bleachers, which could be moved on large caster wheels. The basketball court was filled with gym mats and pillows. Folding chairs and tables were set up throughout the building. This was where they slept.

Colton looked through the bleachers and saw Viper Rex sitting on the front row of the permanent seats. His leg was outstretched and bleeding profusely. He'd cut his pants leg off and was in the process of bandaging his gunshot wound to the upper thigh, using a tee shirt and duct tape.

His groans masked the sound of Colton and Faber's approach. Using hand signals, Colton sent Faber to the far end of the gym to take a position with a clear line of sight to the head of COBRA. Colton moved behind the scorekeeper's table located at the center of the court.

He glanced to his left and saw that Faber was just about in position, getting ready to train her rifle on the target. Colton could've opened fire from his position fifty feet away, but he had something to say first.

"You're a real piece of work, pal," said Colton calmly across the empty gym.

Caught by surprise, Viper Rex scrambled for his handgun and dove under the first-row seating. He responded angrily, "Shut up! My men will be back here any minute to put you in the grave!"

"Doubt it." Colton laughed. "They're all dead. That blood is on your hands."

Viper Rex was kicking at the lantern with his good leg, attempting to turn off the light. He couldn't reach it.

Colton continued. "Let me guess. You prefer to live in the shadows—do your dirty work under the cover of darkness. You're a big man when you're surrounded by guns and mean-looking thugs."

"Shut your mouth, or I'll shut it for you!" He fired several rounds wildly into the air, one of which struck the scoreboard over Colton's head, raining shards of glass onto the bleachers behind him.

Colton wasn't done. "Every despot has a false cause to rally his criminal buddies around. You let your racist beliefs cause the deaths of every one of those men out there. You call yourself King of the Vipers. You're nothing more than a criminal, low-life piece of crap."

"Shut up!"

"You spew all this hatred, demanding atonement and justice, when you're surrounded by people willing to die for you. Let's see what you're made of. Crawl out from behind your phony name, *Viper Rex*, you disgraceful coward, and accept your justice!"

BOOM!

The gunshot reverberated off the walls. The bullet found its mark. Justice was served to Viper Rex—by his own hand.

CHAPTER 36

DAY THIRTEEN
Noon, September 21
HPA Meeting House
Trimble Rd. & Lynnwood Blvd.
Belle Meade, Tennessee

Colton was evolving into something he'd never imagined—a killer without compunction. How could he reconcile taking another man's life with his faith? It has been said that there are no atheists in foxholes. Facing mortal danger had brought many men to prayer. In the aftermath of battle, even those with the strongest faith could become spiritually broken.

A memorial cemetery was created on the vacant lot across from the HPA meeting house. Some of the residents uprooted a white picket fence and transplanted it around the gravesites. Makeshift headstones were created out of scrap plywood and paint. They weren't granite, but were made with love and appreciation nonetheless.

Colton fought back a wave of emotion as he performed the eulogy for the seven brave men who'd lost their lives the day before on Sunnybrook Drive. He tried to provide comfort for the loved ones these brave men left behind. In the process, he grasped for answers to his own questions.

"Nothing in the ordinariness of life can prepare us for the death of our family and friends. Most of us lived in the safety of our homes and careers before the collapse. We'd become desensitized to tragedies suffered by others because they were never dropped at our doorstep. Now, we've all experienced the horror of war.

"All of us realize, when we wake up in the morning, we never know what's going to happen that day. Prepare to be tested again. Don't take for granted the ones you love. Use the graces and the strengths provided by your faith, because you never know when they'll be challenged next."

Colton wiped away the tears. Before he arrived this morning, he'd returned to Mrs. Abercrombie's home and retrieved a picture of her deceased husband off the wall. Within the matted frame was a poem. Although it was often used for the funerals of soldiers who gave their lives in defense of our freedoms, Colton considered it appropriate for these brave men who died defending the safety of every one of their neighbors.

"I would like to conclude with a few words inspired by another of our neighbors who fought for our freedoms."

Colton closed his eyes. Racing through Colton's mind were the bodies he'd buried in the last two weeks. Then he thought about the deaths of his grandfather and his parents and how much he missed them. He needed fortitude to continue, so he asked God for strength.

When he opened his eyes, he looked directly at the tearful faces of Madison and Alex. The only things that mattered stood right in front of him. He'd ask for forgiveness, and he'd reconcile the killings as a necessary evil to protect the ones he loved. But he would never stop loving and protecting them.

Colton took a deep breath and read the poem by Mary Elizabeth Frye.

Do not stand at my grave and weep.
I am not there, I do not sleep.
I am a thousand winds that blow.
I am the diamond glints on snow
I am the sunlight on ripened grain.
I am the gentle autumn rain.
When you awaken in the mornings hush,
I am the swift uplifting rush
of quiet birds in circled flight,
I am the soft stars that shine at night.

Do not stand at my grave and cry,
I am not there, I did not die.

"Rest in peace my friends, and may God be with you. Amen."

CHAPTER 37

DAY THIRTEEN
3:00 p.m., September 21
Ryman Residence
Belle Meade, Tennessee

After two weeks, the neighbors began to embrace their mortality and the inevitable future. Most of them had reached a turning point in which they'd adopted a survival mind-set or they'd accepted their fate. Emotions were taken out of the decision-making process. In a calm, retrospective way, they were choosing life or death. The path his neighbors followed was personal to them and their situation.

Rusty and Karen Kaplan stopped by the Rymans' home to say their goodbyes. Like the Youngs before them and so many other neighbors after yesterday's confrontation, they'd determined the neighborhood was no longer safe.

"Rusty, I'm not gonna try to talk you out of this because I understand where you're coming from," started Colton. "But the feedback I'm receiving from folks is not good. The FEMA facilities are a mirage. They're nothing more than a massive warehousing effort by the government to get us off the streets while they try to restore order to the city."

Rusty symbolically handed Colton the keys to their home, effectively ending the debate. Karen looked at Colton with a look of defeat and resignation. It was the same look he'd received this afternoon during the burial and the brief meeting of the HPA afterward.

"I've heard the rumors too, Colton," said Rusty. "During the … well, yesterday, one of the neighbors returned from 100 Oaks severely beaten. He got into a brawl over food rations. It's been said the personnel running these camps are hoarding food for their cronies. Those who don't play ball, like the fella yesterday, get transferred to a more secure FEMA Camp on Old Briley Parkway that has supposedly been in place for years."

Colton pleaded his case. If they left, his block of Harding Place would be abandoned except for his family. "I know. I've heard those rumors too. I wish you guys would please reconsider. We've established perimeter security. More people are armed now. Despite our losses, I think I've developed some comradery among the neighbors that we didn't have before. We can bind together and get—"

"It's better for us to go there and have a chance than stay here and get killed," interrupted Karen. "Tell Madison and Alex goodbye. I'm sure we'll all be back together soon enough. Let's go, Rusty."

She started to pull Rusty's arm to leave, but he smiled and stopped to shake Colton's hand. "It'll get better soon. Hold down the fort until we get back."

Colton bit his tongue—until it bled! *Hold down the fort?* He was furious with Rusty. Yesterday, he'd risked his life and seven men had died attempting to protect all of the neighbors, including those who didn't participate—like Rusty Kaplan. Now he was asking Colton to continue to risk his life for the Kaplan Fort. *If everybody is leaving, what was the point of yesterday?*

Colton handed the keys back to Rusty. "Be careful. I have my own family and fort to look after and protect. Here, you keep the keys to your *fort.*" Colton turned and walked back towards his house, utterly disgusted.

CHAPTER 38

DAY THIRTEEN
5:00 p.m., September 21
Ryman Residence
Belle Meade, Tennessee

Alex ran down the hill to catch up with her mom and dad. She'd retrieved four grocery totes from the pantry to haul any seeds or gardening supplies they might find in the O'Malleys' home or greenhouse. The O'Malleys were avid gardeners, and it puzzled the Rymans after their first scavenging attempt in the abandoned home that seeds weren't stored somewhere.

Alex was impressed with her mom, who two weeks ago was planning a Friday night party for her dad's friends. Today, she was wearing a black tank top, sunglasses, and was holding an AR-15. Alex immediately thought of Sarah Connor, the character in *The Terminator* movies.

"I'm ready, Daddy," said Alex as she handed him two of the fabric totes.

Out of habit, they both instinctively looked both ways before crossing the street. They decided to start in the back because they both felt they had been fairly thorough inside the house the first time. Alex stood watch on the sidewalk.

For the next half hour, they rummaged through the O'Malleys' greenhouse and garage. They found a few more hand tools, including a hand rake, a whisk broom, and a pair of Fiskars pruning shears. Colton grabbed another funnel out of the garage and a bottle of Roundup. Alex picked up a well-worn copy of *Square Foot Gardening.*

Even if they found the seeds, it didn't mean they'd know how to grow anything.

Alex started thumbing through the book while she waited for her dad to search the garage attic. She found some information on the types of seeds to use and where to store them. The author wrote that the refrigerator was best, but any cool, dry location like a root cellar would be sufficient.

They'd checked the refrigerator previously, so she started to think of a cool, dry place. She walked around the backyard, looking for a root cellar. Nothing. Her dad emerged from the garage with some more fishing gear and a telescope.

"Cool!" exclaimed Alex as she ran to check it out. She dusted it off and revealed the brand. "Wow! It's a Celestron. Good find, Daddy!"

"You're welcome. I'm sure the O'Malleys would be proud for you to give it a good home. Did you find anything?"

"Not really, except for this book," replied Alex. She handed it to him without taking her attention away from the telescope.

"I guess we'll head back," announced Colton.

"Wait. Daddy, the book said you should store seeds in a cool, dry place like a root cellar. I looked around the yard but couldn't find one."

They both looked around the yard, searching for a clue. Suddenly, Alex handed her dad the telescope and headed around the side of the house. The O'Malleys had installed a series of stepping-stones leading from the elevated deck around the corner. She remembered seeing a small entry door to the home's crawl space.

Alex found the three-foot-square door and slid the bolt latch. As she opened the door, a burst of cool air hit her face. The setting sun illuminated the interior, which contained rows of handmade shelves containing Ziploc bags marked by years. Each bag contained an envelope that was clearly marked with a different vegetable name and variety.

"Winner!" exclaimed Alex as she crawled under the house on all fours.

"What did you find?" asked Colton. Alex responded by handing out an old wooden soft drink crate marked Royal Crown Cola. It was full of seeds. "This is fantastic, Alex!"

"You have no idea," came the reply from deeper inside the crawl space. Alex began to shove more crates toward the entrance, which were quickly retrieved by Colton.

After eight crates containing two dozen packets each were extricated from the cramped space, Alex collapsed in the grass and began to thumb through the labeled Ziplocs.

"They all read heirloom seeds," said Colton.

"What's that mean?" asked Alex.

"I don't know," replied Colton. "Maybe they've been passed down through the generations?"

Alex shrugged and pulled some of the packets out of the bags.

"Corn, cucumber, pumpkin, tomato, and watermelon," she read aloud. "Daddy, watermelon!"

"Dang straight!" replied Colton. She was beaming, not only because of the find, but because she made her dad smile. He hadn't smiled much lately.

"C'mon," started Alex, looking around nervously. "Let's get these home before somebody sees us."

The two loaded up their vegetable garden supplies and hurried to a waiting Madison, who helped carry the crates to the house. At the top of the driveway, Alex realized she forgot her telescope.

"Here, Daddy. Take these. I forgot my telescope. I'll be right back."

"Alex, wait," Colton shouted after her. "Don't go alone."

But it was too late, and she was already crossing the street.

Alex ran to the backyard and retrieved the telescope. She was walking toward the front yard when she heard squeaking sounds. Alex immediately looked down the street and saw people headed her way, forcing her to freeze, unable to move, much less run.

It wasn't out of fear, but rather shock. Coming towards her was a group of four people. An elderly woman in a pink bathrobe rode in a wheelchair with a paisley suitcase on her lap. Another woman in her late thirties was pushing the wheelchair while pulling a suitcase on wheels. An older boy was urging a wheelbarrow along the street with a nearly flat tire, which contained the elderly woman's walker, more luggage and some photo albums.

Then she recognized Corey Hart, her classmate from grade school before she entered Davidson Academy. She discovered the source of the loud squeaking sound. Corey was pulling an old Radio Flyer Town & Country wagon, the kind with the removable wooden sides.

Alex walked into the middle of the road and saw her dad coming down the front yard in a hurry. "It's okay, Daddy," said Alex, holding her right hand up to slow down his approach. She turned her attention to the group.

"Hey, Corey," said Alex hesitantly.

"Hey, Alex. How's it goin'?"

"Okay, I guess," she replied. "Is this your family?"

Madison had now joined up with Colton, who remained on the sidewalk. She tucked her arm inside of Colton's while Alex reunited with her old friend.

"Yeah, we're going to 100 Oaks," he replied. "We probably waited too long."

Alex looked at the elderly woman and then glanced down the street behind the group. "My name's Alex," she said, extending her hand to shake. The woman, without responding, could barely lift her left hand for Alex to shake it. Her hand was bony and cold to the touch.

"This is my mom and older brother," said Corey.

Alex looked into the sullen, dark eyes of the other two members of the family and then realized some people were missing. She hesitated, not knowing if asking about the others was the right thing to do.

She looked back to Corey, and whispered, "Where are your grandpa and ...?" She couldn't bring herself to finish the question.

"My dad died trying to defend the hardware store from looters. Grandpa died trying to put out the fire the looters set when they were done trashing the place. The whole block is on fire now."

Alex looked to the west and saw the black clouds of smoke through the trees. After the rains of two days ago, they thought the threats from fires would be over. *Apparently not.*

"I'm really sorry, Corey," said Alex. She looked into the distraught faces of both of the Hart widows. She turned her attention to the elderly wife of the nice man who'd helped Alex and her mom at the hardware store just two weeks ago. "I'm sorry, Mrs. Hart. Your husband was a very nice man."

Alex began to cry and Corey gave her a hug. "We've got to get goin', Alex. It's getting late. Hi, Mr. and Mrs. Ryman." He waved as the Radio Flyer began to squeak again.

The Rymans stood in the middle of Harding Place for ten minutes in silence—watching the remainder of the Hart family until they disappeared in the distance. Alex looked around their street. They were completely alone. There were no kids playing in the yards. No moms were pushing strollers on the sidewalk. No cars were returning from soccer practice. There was only silence.

Alex looked to the sky, and then she heard a faint sound. Her eyes adjusted to the bright setting sun until she caught a glimpse of a flock of geese making their way south in a V formation—migrating to a place where they could find food and a better place to nest.

CHAPTER 39

DAY FOURTEEN
6:00 p.m., September 22
Ryman Residence
Belle Meade, Tennessee

Earlier, Colton had returned from the HPA meeting, which he attended alone. Less than a dozen people showed up. Even Shane Wren was missing. Despite eradicating the COBRA gang, looters were still present in the neighborhood. Two homes were ransacked on Iroquois, only two blocks north of them. In the exclusive neighborhood of Northumberland, squatters—who were former residents of the 100 Oaks FEMA camp—had evicted the residents and taken over their homes. They were now going house to house in search of food and supplies—sweeping through the neighborhood like locusts.

Time was running out on them as fires burned out of control on the other side of Belle Meade Country Club. The sky to their west was filled with dense, black smoke, which obscured the sunset tonight.

Madison believed that everything happened for a reason. Things went wrong so you could appreciate them when they were right. You believed lies, so you eventually learned to trust no one but your family. Sometimes good things fell apart so better things could come together. The Rymans were at a turning point in their lives in which the brief moments they spent smiling with the ones they loved meant the most.

"Hey, gorgeous," said Colton as he gave Madison a hug around the waist. "Watcha got planned for dinner? Oatmeal? Perhaps beans and rice with a touch of paprika?"

"Nope," she replied. She handed him a stack of china. "Here. Set the dining room table."

"Whoa, fancy!" Colton laughed. "What's the occasion? Did I miss our anniversary?"

"No, but you better not forget it," admonished Madison. "Take these candleholders in there too and these cloth napkins."

Alex entered the kitchen after a nap. She'd taken the sight of the Hart family pretty hard and had gone straight to her room after the encounter. Madison and Colton agreed to give her some space and extra time to rest.

"Hi, honey," said Madison as she gave her daughter a kiss on the cheek. "Help your daddy set the table while I bring in the food."

Madison carried a woven rattan serving tray to the pool house and retrieved the food, which she was keeping warm on the Camp Chef grill. Before she came in, she took a quick glance around the backyard to make sure nobody was drawn to their home by the smell of cooking.

"Here we go," started Madison. "We have green beans with almonds, baby new potatoes with garlic and peppercorns, carrots, and everybody's favorite—grilled Spam topped with pineapple slices."

"Holy moly," exclaimed Alex.

"I agree," said Colton. "Hey, is that wine in the stemware?"

"No, sir. Pineapple juice."

"I'll take it," said Colton.

The Rymans sat at the table and followed a tradition that used to be commonplace in homes across America. The days of families enjoying meals together were gone. The days of saying the blessing before meals was long gone.

"Bless, O Lord, this food when others are hungry; this drink when others are thirsty; our family when others are lonely. Through Christ we pray, Amen."

"Amen."

"Amen."

They passed their plates around and enjoyed their first meal together that resembled a family dinner since the power went out. It felt good and they actually laughed about what they would've been doing right now if the power remained on. Colton would be working late at the office. Alex would be buried in her very popular social media accounts. Madison would be thumbing through a magazine, waiting for her favorite television show to come on.

"One thing about the apocalypse—" Colton chuckled as he finished off his last bite of Spam with a slight belch "—we're all together. Seriously, is there anything better than this?"

Madison reached out and tenderly grasped his hand. "Nope," she said, smiling.

"Well, perhaps Katz's deli," chimed in Colton, earning a slug to the arm from his wife, the chef.

"Maybe golf," said Alex dryly. They all laughed.

"Well, maybe we can find a spot on a golf course," said Madison with a tone of seriousness in her voice.

"Ha-ha, Mom," started Alex. "My golf course is on fire."

"Exactly," said Madison, pushing away from the table and walking into the kitchen. She returned with a notepad and pen. "I think it's time for us to leave."

"What? Really?" asked Colton.

"Yep," replied Madison with confidence. She laid the notepad in front of her and leaned back in her chair. "I'm sure many people have headed for the hills, so to speak. I think the preppers call it bugging out. Then there are others like us, who, to an extent, hold out for as long as their home is still standing. But there comes a turning point where you have to decide if that continues to make sense."

"Whadya mean, Mom?"

"There is never a clear-cut answer in most cases, but it seems to me our decision is being made each and every day. Things are not going to get better around here. I think we're reducing our options by waiting. We should leave on our terms, not when our hands are forced by someone else."

"When?" asked Alex.

"I fixed this nice meal for us tonight for a reason," replied Madison. "We need to leave now. We need to pack the truck and go."

"But where? We don't know what to expect out there," said Alex.

"That's true, honey," replied Colton. "But we do know what to expect here—gunfights, looters, out-of-control fires, and ultimately—the FEMA camp."

Madison picked up the list and slid it over to Colton. "I've been thinking about this for days. Here's a list of pros and cons. We have enough food to last a month. If we stay here, it will be increasingly dangerous to make your runs. Why? Everybody is doing the same thing. We've got to get into a rural area where we can trade for food and, in the spring, grow our own—thanks to the O'Malleys."

Colton ran his finger down the list. "I didn't realize how much stuff we've accumulated. It's a pretty good list, Madison."

"It is. I thought about the EMP book I bought and went back to review the checklist in the back. We've done pretty good on our beans, Band-Aids, and bullets. Our weak spot is shelter, a safer place to live where we can start over."

Alex spoke up. "Back to my question. Where can we go?"

"I've got a pretty good idea for a plan A that we can talk about while we're packing."

"Is there a plan B?"

"I'll let you know on our way to plan A. C'mon!"

CHAPTER 40

DAY FOURTEEN
11:00 p.m., September 22
Ryman Residence
Belle Meade, Tennessee

Having an emergency evacuation plan was critical during any survival situation. After a collapse event, having a plan of action would help make the decision-making process easier as to where to go and what to take. The Rymans weren't preppers, but they were learning by applying common sense and via the crash course in preparedness they'd received in the last fourteen days.

Colton pulled out their map book and foldout maps and studied the plan with the girls. They would head for Shiloh, Tennessee, on the banks of the Tennessee River, approximately one hundred fifty miles to their southwest. Colton's longtime client Jake Allen had a vacation home there.

A few years ago, the Rymans spent a couple of weeks with Jake, his wife, Emily, and their son, Chase, who was now seventeen. Colton didn't know whether the Allens would be at the Shiloh ranch. Their permanent residence was halfway between Springfield and Branson, Missouri, where Jake played with his band at a newly created music venue. Years ago, an elderly man and woman lived on the Shiloh ranch as resident caretakers. Colton hoped the Allens were there, but if not, the caretakers might allow them to stay—at least for a while.

Over the next five hours after dinner, the Ryman household was bustling with activity. Everyone was excited about the prospect of getting out of the city. Colton was upset with himself for not broaching the subject earlier. Madison and Alex each had their seminal moment, an epiphany, after the events of the last few days. There was never a doubt they'd turned the page on this chapter of their life, and it was time to move on. For Colton, it was merely a matter of numbers. If they stayed in the city, they'd be outnumbered by the bad guys. It was time to go.

They packed everything of value for survival in this world without power. Following the beans, Band-Aids and bullets axiom was the easy part. Loading up all of the other supplies and tools they'd accumulated was more difficult.

The sixty-inch cargo carrier was affixed to the truck's hitch. Colton stacked the generator and extra gasoline inside of its rails. Then, he crammed the power tools in every available space and tied it all together with bungee cords. Colton covered the entire bundle with a tarp procured from the cable repair van.

Inside the Wagoneer, every duffle bag from the house was stuffed with medical supplies, alternative lighting, and their camping gear. Clothing was the subject of debate, especially with a fifteen-year-old girl. Their focus was on comfort, warmth, modesty, and blending in. Madison and Alex were careful not to choose any clothing items that might be considered provocative. In a post-apocalyptic world without rule of law, some men might be quick to violate acceptable boundaries. There would be no need to encourage them. All of them focused on athletic wear with as many pairs of sneakers and cotton socks as they could find. Each of them packed their most comfortable pair of western boots and stuffed them full with socks. Finally, accessories—including gloves, scarves, hats, sweatshirts and coats—were crammed into every nook and cranny.

Colton used a six-inch PVC pipe retrieved from the house being remodeled and stuffed the fishing gear inside. He sealed the ends with beach towels, Saran Wrap, and duct tape. He took one of their comforters and wrapped their shovels, hoes, rakes, and axes they'd found during their scavenging expeditions. These were wrapped with duct tape and bungeed to the roof rack of the Wagoneer.

Madison secured all of their important legal documents like birth certificates, passports, licenses, deeds and financial documents in waterproof, one-gallon Ziploc bags. She also gathered up all of their photographs and special mementos. Just because they were leaving Harding Place didn't mean they were leaving their lives and memories behind.

Weapons would be kept handy in the front, where the three of them would occupy the bench seat. The remainder of the interior was packed to the ceiling with everything imaginable to help them reestablish their lives elsewhere until they could return.

Alex agreed to stand watch all night since she got so much sleep earlier in the day. As an exhausted Colton and Madison struggled to climb the stairs, he was optimistic their last night in their home would be a peaceful one.

CHAPTER 41

DAY FIFTEEN
6:00 a.m., September 23
Ryman Residence
Belle Meade, Tennessee

The last night was uneventful, and Alex woke up her parents from a deep sleep. She used the last of the propane fuel to make a pot of coffee and warm up some blueberry Pop-Tarts. The family was mostly silent as the reality of leaving set in. After they finished off the coffee and used the bathroom, Colton packed up the grill and announced they were ready.

The three of them made one final walk-through as they said goodbye to the home where Alex had lived most of her life. She knew leaving home was a part of growing up and that her time to venture out into the world was coming, but not under these circumstances.

Madison shed several tears as she closed the kitchen door behind them. Colton opened the garage door, revealing the trophy received for the most cleverly negotiated deal in his career—the Jeep Wagoneer. This old truck was their lifeline now. It was their means to a new life far away from the post-apocalyptic madness of the big city.

Colton eased the truck out of the garage and worked his way down the driveway until he had to veer through the front yard to avoid the Suburban. As he wheeled his way around the landscaping, all three of them looked toward the west where fire danced above the tall oak trees. Reminiscent of a scene from *Gone with the Wind*, the magnificent antebellum homes of Belle Meade were in flames.

Madison began to sob now. "Will we ever be able to return?"

"What about our things?" asked Alex.

"Having somewhere to live is home. Having someone to love is family. All we need is right here in this front seat—our family." With that, Colton drove onto the road and led the Ryman family on a new adventure and to a new home.

They'd reached their turning point—a point of no return.

THANK YOU FOR READING ZERO HOUR!

If you enjoyed it, I'd be grateful if you'd take a moment to write a short review (just a few words are needed) and post it on Amazon. Amazon uses complicated algorithms to determine what books are recommended to readers. Sales are, of course, a factor, but so are the quantities of reviews my books get. By taking a few seconds to leave a review, you help me out, and also help new readers learn about my work.

And before you go...

SIGN UP for Bobby Akart's mailing list to receive special offers, bonus content, and you'll be the first to receive news about new releases.

eepurl.com/bYqq3L

VISIT Amazon.com/BobbyAkart for more information on his next project, as well as his completed words: the Doomsday series, the Yellowstone series, the Lone Star series, the Pandemic series, the Blackout series, the Boston Brahmin series and the Prepping for Tomorrow series totaling nearly forty novels, including over thirty Amazon #1 Bestsellers in forty-plus fiction and nonfiction genres.

Visit Bobby Akart's website for informative blog entries on preparedness, writing, and a behind-the-scenes look into his novels.

BobbyAkart.com

READ ON FOR A BONUS EXCERPT from

TURNING POINT

Book Three of The Blackout Series

TURNING
POINT
BEST SELLING AUTHOR
BOBBY AKART
BOOK THREE OF THE BLACKOUT SERIES

PROLOGUE

November 1976
McNairy County
Adamsville, Tennessee

Not many people knew the real story of Buford Pusser, the long-time sheriff of McNairy County in southwest Tennessee. Even fewer knew the story of his daughter, Betty Jean Pusser.

This is the tale of one of the darkest days in the history of the tiny town of Adamsville, Tennessee. The town, and all of McNairy County, had seen its share of crime and punishment—administered by a man some called a hero, and others called part of the problem, Sheriff Buford Pusser.

The city's worst day began quietly enough when a used-car salesman discovered one of his cars missing, an anonymous-looking black Ford. The theft was strange, because the boxy '62 Fairlane was about the least valuable car on the lot, so ordinary it seemed invisible—like an undercover police car or a getaway car.

It was the morning after Election Day in 1976 and the peanut farmer from Plains, Georgia, had defeated that Yankee Gerald Ford, much to the delight of democrats across the south. The car salesman's head was swollen from too much 'shine and celebration, but he managed to open his dealership on time nonetheless.

The day ended quietly, too, with a series of muted popping noises, much like the sound of a newspaper rolled loosely into a fly swatter and slapped on a tabletop. Few people heard those nine innocuous pops, and those who did never spoke of them. Yet those sounds would destroy a family, alter countless lives, transform a town, and create a monster. Little would remain the same in Adamsville, Tennessee, or the surrounding counties, in their wake.

Between those two events that fateful day, Clarence and Wanda Tindle lived as they always had, taking no special precautions, exhibiting few outward fears. Adamsville was a quiet town now, following Sheriff Pusser's tumultuous time in office. Clarence went to the law office he'd occupied for nearly twenty years, where he'd served McNairy County as a criminal defense lawyer. Wanda, as always, worked much of the day on her one great obsession—exposing McNairy County's legendary corruption, in her capacity as the editor of the *Independent Appeal* newspaper. On the surface, they were above reproach and widely respected in McNairy County.

During that last day, Clarence also found time to walk his German shepherd, joke with his law partner—a staunch Republican—about the election, get his thick shock of graying hair cut at the local barbershop, and gas up his new Buick Estate station wagon in preparation for a trip Friday to Memphis.

Wanda spent the better part of that Wednesday shopping for clothes for her increasingly round five-foot frame, buying one of those newfangled microcassette voice recorders, and planning a United Daughters of the Confederacy convention she was chairing in December. At one time or another during the day, she told people she had contacted the FBI about the harassment they'd been receiving from a private investigator who'd been digging around in the death of the illustrious former sheriff since his accident in 1974.

Sheriff Pusser was a legend in McNairy County. As the sheriff of this small rural county along the Mississippi-Tennessee state line, he'd become a one-man army fighting gambling, prostitution, and moonshining operations, which had run rampant during his term in the late sixties.

His life gave rise to several books and movies, and one very large conspiracy. You see, Buford Pusser died in August 1974 after his Corvette careened off Highway 64 at a high rate of speed, and he was ejected from the car before it caught fire.

Moments later, his daughter, thirteen-year old Betty Jean, came upon the scene while on her way home with friends. She found her pa holding on to life, and with his last, dying breath Pusser whispered in Betty Jean's ear, "They finally got me."

Although an autopsy was not performed, the state trooper working the accident, who later became the sheriff of McNairy County, took a sample of Pusser's blood. The hospital released the results stating his blood-alcohol level was in excess of the legal limit. That state trooper was Clarence Tindle's younger brother.

As the rumors ran rampant throughout the county, accusations were leveled at Trooper Tindle. The Tindles fought back with a hit piece exposé on Pusser's dealings while sheriff, using Wanda Tindle's position at the newspaper as a bully pulpit.

Pusser's mother hired a small-time private detective, who quickly developed a working theory that the Tindles had the motive and opportunity to sabotage Pusser's Corvette, resulting in his death. Clarence was tied to the crime figures who Pusser tried to put away. Wanda relentlessly pursued corruption charges against Pusser. And former Trooper Tindle, the sole investigating officer, declared his intentions to become sheriff. The private detective was paid handsomely for this theory—to the tune of over one hundred thousand dollars.

The war of words continued for over a year, during which time the hostilities finally simmered down—until Election Day, 1976. Trooper Tindle became Sheriff Tindle on that date to much fanfare throughout the county.

This enraged Buford Pusser's mother, who was convinced the Tindle family was responsible for her beloved son's death. She exploded in anger in front of her orphaned grandchild, now fifteen-year-old Betty Jean, who took it to heart.

On that fateful Wednesday night, Clarence and his brother, newly elected Sheriff Tindle, shared a drink in celebration of his victory. Wanda went upstairs to draw a bath and soak her weary bones.

While Wanda relaxed with a glass of wine, she thought she heard a faint knock, but then the boys started laughing, so she disregarded it. It was probably several minutes later, nobody would know for sure, when she heard, faintly, the first popping noise.

She then thought she heard a vague sound of movement in the living room, followed by more *pop—pop—pop* sounds. There went Clarence again, swatting flies with a newspaper. They were both drunk and probably couldn't hit the broadside of a barn with their best effort. She laughed to herself as she finished off the glass, allowing the warm wine to soak into her bloodstream.

It was several minutes later when the bathroom door creaked open and frail, impish Betty Jean Pusser walked in, carrying a .22-caliber Ruger with a black tube silencer sitting fat and obscene on the lip of the barrel. Wanda attempted to cover her naked body with her arms as young Betty Jean pointed the gun at Wanda's head. Betty Jean wasn't shaking from nervousness. Her eyes were dark, lifeless. She only allowed herself a slight smile as she gently pulled the trigger.

Wanda Tindle never heard those last four quiet pops. Consciousness, dreams, and fear were all obliterated before the sound of that first silenced shot stopped echoing off the tiled bathroom walls.

And the day ended as quietly as it had begun, with a nondescript Ford Fairlane disappearing down a deserted street to a faraway rock quarry and its final resting place at the bottom of a murky lake.

Everyone's life contains a seminal event, a turning point that shapes who they are and how they interact with their fellow man. Betty Jean Pusser's turning point came that day at the age of fifteen.

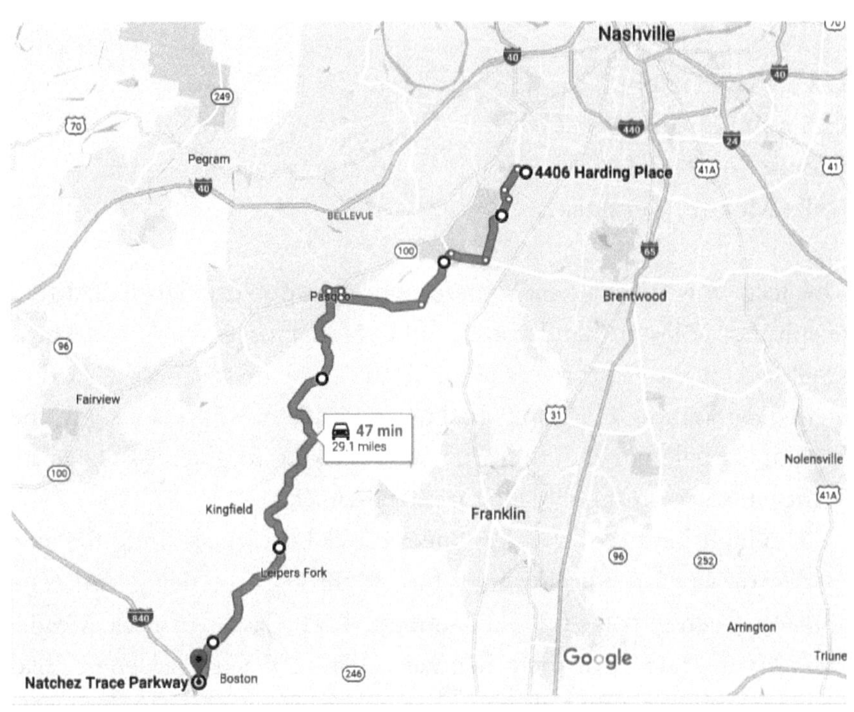
Nashville
Pegram
BELLEVUE
4406 Harding Place
Brentwood
Fairview
47 min
29.1 miles
Nolensville
Kingfield
Franklin
Leipers Fork
Arrington
Google
Triune
Natchez Trace Parkway
Boston

CHAPTER 1

DAY FIFTEEN
6:15 a.m., September 23
Chickering Road
Belle Meade, Tennessee

The Jeep Wagoneer's headlights caught a cardboard sign nailed to a telephone pole—a handwritten sign—*The End is Nigh*. Darkness swallowed it and Colton was left with the sense he was on the road to eternal damnation. His family had taken God's most precious gift, the lives of his fellow men. He wasn't sure if asking forgiveness would be sufficient to avoid the fate in store for them.

The high beams of the Wagoneer clawed the grass along the side of the tree-lined road, plowing a furrow through the dewy landscape so neon green in color it looked unnatural. The lawns of Belle Meade, which were once pristinely maintained by efficient gardeners, had become overgrown and unruly.

Everything Colton knew, or thought he knew, about Nashville and Belle Meade had been erased by the end of the world as he knew it. Two weeks after the devastating solar storm that caused the collapse of the nation's power grid, his family had gone from days filled with work, social activity for Madison, and school for Alex, to a post-apocalyptic dystopia where death had become commonplace.

The Rymans' worldly goods were crammed into the Wagoneer—memories of the past and the tools to survive an unknown future. Colton reached for Madison, who'd remained quiet since their departure from Harding Place. He gave his devoted wife's hand a squeeze to gain a reaction from her. Madison turned her face to look at Colton, managed a smile, and wiped away the last of her tears.

"Are we there yet?" She laughed, letting out some emotion. They'd been on the road for only fifteen minutes.

"I wish," chimed in Alex from the backseat. Alex had been remarkable as the world of a teenage girl crashed around her. She was very mature and logical for her age. Daily activities for Alex revolved around her school and love for golf, which had both been ripped from her life.

She'd also killed a man. After an initial period of shock, Alex had become incredibly at peace with the shooting, which was clearly in self-defense. Colton wasn't sure whether he should be proud of her acceptance of taking another man's life, or concerned that his daughter might be harboring feelings that needed to be released.

In any event, there wasn't time to explore the mind's inner workings. A lot had happened in the last fourteen days and he needed to focus on the task at hand—safety and a new home for the Ryman family.

Colton rolled down the window of the 1969 Jeep Wagoneer using the hand crank. Fresh morning air filled the truck as the sun slowly began to rise to their left. Another hand-printed sign came into view, this one riddled with bullet holes—REPENT. FINAL WARNING.

The Rymans had reached a turning point and were forced to make a decision. The neighborhood had collapsed around them. Fires were burning out of control to their west. Gangs were infiltrating the streets and homes to their north. Families were abandoning their residences in droves, seeking the utopian comfort and security of the FEMA camps established throughout metro Nashville. The Rymans, however, chose the potential safety of the countryside over a certain life of gunfights and scavenging in the city.

"It's really quiet, isn't it?" replied Colton, attempting to make small talk as they drove into a future where nothing was sure and anything was possible. "It's been a while since we took a road trip. Kinda nice without traffic."

Neither Madison nor Alex provided a response. Colton continued to ease his way along Chickering Drive as the Rymans headed southwest out of town—destination Shiloh, Tennessee, on the banks of the Tennessee River.

The concept of hitting the open road was almost romantic in its scope. We liked to think of everything going crazy in the world being left behind as we head out into the presumed serenity of the farms and desolate countryside.

But just like life, a winding road contained unknown perils and troubles. You never knew where the bend in the road might take you.

As he wheeled the Wagoneer through several abandoned cars, a downed tree limb blocked their progress. Colton approached slowly, scanning the sides of the road for indications of trouble. The sun was rising and the morning light allowed him better visibility. There didn't appear to be any other signs of life, so Colton slipped his gun into his paddle holster and shut off the engine.

"Wait here. I've got this," said Colton to Madison and Alex. He exited the Wagoneer and stopped, stunned by his surroundings.

This stretch of road was relatively uninhabited. Once outside the car, the silence was shattered. Surprised by the sheer magnitude of the sounds, Colton stood and listened.

A choir, a community, no, a nation of frogs sang from the darkness still engulfing the woods surrounding him. Wide and deep, the croaking critters chirped and chortled from every direction. Croaks both rough and guttural filled the air, buoyed by a mixture of higher tones from other frog species.

Big croaks. Big doggone frogs, Colton thought.

Then, in unison, as if directed by a conductor, they stopped.

Silence.

Intuitively, Colton immediately crouched down next to the Wagoneer. He considered leaving, but Colton hesitated to start the engine for fear of being discovered. He peered over the driver's door and held a finger up to his lips. He mouthed the words to his girls—*be quiet!*

A crack of a tree branch and the sounds of heavy steps coming from the woods to his left caught his attention. He scrambled to the front of the Wagoneer, keeping the hood of the large truck between him and the potential threat.

Already? Really? We've only been gone half an hour!

Colton pulled his sidearm and released the safety. He trained the weapon on a clearing in the woods from which the sounds emanated. He was ready as the sounds grew louder. *Heavy steps. Not attempting to hide their approach.* Colton was sweating, slightly obstructing his vision.

Bursting into the clearing from the woods, two chestnut and black quarter horses trotted towards him and then abruptly turned down the shoulder of the road toward the south. Off they went in a slow gallop, rounding the curve as they took life's hurdles in stride.

Colton's body relaxed and he leaned toward the hood of the Wagoneer, intentionally bumping his head on the hood to restart his heart, which had momentarily taken a break during the stressful arrival of the horses.

He stood and began to laugh nervously. Madison rolled down the passenger window.

"Hey, Colt, do I need to get you another pair of pants?" she asked, laughing. Unconsciously, Colton reached behind and felt the seat of his jeans, just in case.

"Very funny," he replied. Colton holstered his weapon and efficiently removed the obstructing tree limb from their path.

As he did, Colton thought about the fact that any game plan always looked good on paper, but rarely did it turn out that way. Murphy's Law, *whoever Murphy was*, stated that anything that could go wrong, would go wrong and probably at the worst possible moment.

Colton reached for the handle of the truck just as the conductor struck up the Croakin' Frog Jamboree.

Big croaks.

CHAPTER 2

DAY FIFTEEN
6:45 a.m., September 23
Chickering Road
Forest Hills, Tennessee

Alex leaned against the door and stared out the window toward Harpeth Hills Golf Course on her right. She'd miss golf. Obviously, there wasn't room in the Wagoneer to bring her clubs. She wasn't even sure if there was a course near Shiloh—not that it mattered.

She'd miss some of her friends, although she'd learned early on in high school that many were conniving backstabbers. The night the lights went out, Daddy had warned her and Mom about the depravity of man. Alex didn't find the need to remind him that she'd learned about the depravity of her fellow teenagers years ago.

Alex would miss Disney movies and her favorite reality television shows—*Survivor* and *Big Brother*. She'd miss chocolate and Facebook. But that was about it. Seeing Harpeth Hills devoid of golfers was a grim reminder of a life without her favorite pastime.

As the sun rose, so did the walkers. No, not the walkers referenced on *The Walking Dead*, one of her favorite shows. Alex never could figure out why the characters on *The Walking Dead* didn't call them zombies. That was what they were, and that was also what these people looked like as well.

Her dad slowed as refugees began to appear on both sides of the road. Once in a while, one would approach the truck, holding out their hands, looking for some type of mercy. The family had talked about this the night before. There would come a time when they'd be able to help others in need. First, they had to protect themselves.

Alex studied the walkers. There appeared to be two types of post-apocalyptic refugees—those who were marginally prepared and those who were not. The way they were dressed was one indicator. The way their skin hung on their degenerating bodies was another. Those who'd gone longer without food appeared drunk, at times staggering toward the truck as they turned to look at the odd sight of a moving vehicle.

Alex began to imagine every man, woman, and child leaving Nashville, fleeing the apocalyptic carnage of the city in search of shelter, food, and safety. As the heavily populated areas of South Nashville succumbed to anarchy and out-of-control fires, neighbors became survivors, but eventually, survivors sought other options besides their homes and became refugees.

Either the sound of their approaching vehicle or the rising sun caused the refugees to awaken. Faces of women and children peered through the windows of abandoned cars. Whole families living in lean-to shelters made up of cardboard boxes and tarps poked their heads out to take a look. Harpeth Hills golf course had become a tent city.

"Are we refugees, Daddy?" asked Alex as she continued to wonder at the masses of people who'd congregated here.

"I guess so," he replied. "In a way, anyone who's displaced from their home due to a catastrophe would be considered a refugee."

"Like after Hurricane Katrina?" asked Alex.

"Exactly, although many of those people were more like evacuees because they had homes to return to," responded Madison. She turned to look at Alex in the backseat. "I think a refugee is someone that's permanently displaced."

"Like us," said Alex, who began to get emotional at the thought of never being able to return home.

"Not necessarily, Allie-Cat," said Colton. "We had to leave for our safety, just like the evacuees from Katrina. When they returned to their homes, they didn't know what to expect. We're in the same situation."

"That's right, honey," said Madison. "We'll return home one day when things return to normal."

Alex pondered this thought for a moment, doubting that her mother was certain of her own words. They'd taken the steps to leave the doors to the house unlocked but closed. Madison had left all of the cupboard doors open and the closet doors ajar. They had even created the appearance that their home had already been looted. With a little luck, any thieves would move through quickly, realize there was nothing of survival value, and go on to the next home. Her daddy thought this would increase their chances of having something to return to if their home wasn't consumed by the fires.

"Honey, most people are creatures of habit," Madison continued. "They'll only move if something forces them to. Some people, like these folks on the side of the road, left before us. They didn't have any place to go. They just needed to get away from what was happening all around them."

Alex continued to stare at the makeshift tent city as Colton continued the conversation. "It's like your mom said, humans are habitual. We're also creatures of comfort. In most emergencies, people will not want to leave their homes. Kinda like us. Something has to dislodge them, and when it does, it may be too late.

"When the power grid went down and the water stopped working, a lot of folks, even our neighbors, thought the government would get things up and running again. They didn't accept reality right away and used up their resources like food and water."

"I know," said Alex. "Jimmy Holder told me that some of the neighbors were drinking water out of their hot water heaters and then their toilets. It was gross."

"They were desperate," said Colton. "When those options ran out, they left the city, looking for water, food, shelter and safety."

"Why did they stop here, at a golf course?" asked Alex.

Colton wheeled the Wagoneer through several abandoned cars and turned right onto Old Hickory Boulevard. "We're fortunate to have transportation," he replied. "All of these people got the heck out of Dodge, searching for places to hunt and fish. They'll stay here until something dislodges them again, and then they'll strike out for points farther away from the city."

"They seem to be getting along," observed Alex. The sun was in full view and the day was under way for the refugees. Many stood talking to one another, pointing at the Wagoneer as it eased down the road.

Colton continued. "As time progresses and things get more dangerous, they'll begin to weigh their options. Just like at home, these folks will band together and take the approach that there is strength in numbers."

"Will they become marauders too?"

"Maybe," said Madison. "As we've learned, desperate people will do desperate things. People who've walked this far will realize there aren't enough fish in the pond around here, or notice that it's getting too crowded and dangerous. They'll begin to think the grass is greener somewhere else, causing them to migrate towards the farms or towards a river."

"Unfortunately, they might loot along the way," added Colton. "As this group of refugees walks out of the metropolitan area toward the farms and small towns, they'll branch off the main highway onto small side roads or gravel driveways. Mile after mile after mile, they'll approach the scattered houses and barns off in the distance, searching for food, water, and shelter. They might find them empty or heavily defended. The owners might say *stop*, or *I'll shoot.* Others will simply shoot and ask questions later. That's the risk you run in wandering aimlessly into the countryside."

Alex sat quietly, staring at the sullen faces and starving children as they drove past. The sun was rising and, with it, her apprehension. The vague picture she'd conjured up in her mind last night of farms full of crops and fields teeming with cattle had been replaced with thoughts of locust-like refugees spreading far and wide, creating a bleak and plundered world ravaged by the hungry walkers—dotted with burned-down homes and broken-down vehicles.

She quietly said a prayer thanking God for her parents, and their 1969 Jeep Wagoneer, before she drifted off to sleep.

CHAPTER 3

DAY FIFTEEN
7:15 a.m., September 23
Old Hickory Boulevard
Belle Meade, Tennessee

Madison continued to study the map as they cleared the last cluster of homes along Old Hickory Boulevard. They'd need to take a left up ahead on Vaughn Road, which provided them a direct shot to the Natchez Trace Parkway.

When she'd plotted their route toward Shiloh over the past couple of days, she decided on the Natchez Trace Parkway because it was a relatively direct route and they wouldn't encounter many small towns. What she didn't envision were the temporary towns springing up outside the city. Seeing the number of refugees camped out on the golf course surprised her.

The false alarm caused by the horses and the appearance of the refugees were cause for her to reconsider if this was the right thing to do. Madison knew there would be challenges to face, but the rising sun shed light on the realities of what the Rymans might face along the way.

Madison recalled the words written in the prepping books she'd purchased just before the solar storm hit. *Bugging out* was the terminology used by the preppers. At the time she was reading about the concept, Madison was unaware that Colton had successfully traded a shiny new, but now worthless, Corvette for this partially rusted out hunk of junk.

During those thirty-six hours, Madison first had to come to grips with the threat their family faced if the predictions and possibilities were true. Admittedly, the thought of having to bug out hadn't crossed her mind. Any plan involving leaving their home was murky and, as a result, shoved to the rear of the preparedness planning line. The way she looked at it, the notion of bugging out was simple—grab your stuff and go.

Bugging out was considered a last resort for Madison. Like so many others, she never imagined the threats would escalate to the point her family would be forced out of their home. The rose-colored glasses got ripped away from so many people at once. Tensions were bound to boil over. Somehow, their beautiful city and their once quiet neighborhood had become a field of battle. Decades of pressure and stress had pushed ordinary Americans to the brink, and all it took was one catastrophic event to push them over the edge. Now in hindsight, Madison was amazed her family had lasted in their home as long as they did.

As Colton slowly approached the intersection of Vaughan Road, Madison realized her biggest regret was not having a specific place to bug out to. Jake Allen's ranch in Shiloh seemed like the perfect location, but nobody knew they were coming. Plus, the Rymans only assumed they'd be welcomed in.

Madison leaned forward to focus her view on the upcoming intersection. Ahead were numerous tents set up within the baseball fields, and more than a dozen stalled vehicles along the road slowed their progress. Edwin Warner Park had become a temporary town of its own.

"Turn left here, honey," said Madison. The intersection appeared to be blocked ahead, but Colton improvised by navigating the Wagoneer onto the shoulder and past the grassy baseball diamonds of Heriges Memorial Field.

After the solar storm, their world got much smaller. Their boundaries were limited by the distance they could walk or ride a bike. While the Wagoneer expanded their world, the Rymans quickly learned that the roads were not passable in many instances, like this one.

Madison's mind wandered back to the bug-out process. Madison had learned that the art of prepping was not an exact science. For one thing, predicting when and where a catastrophic event would occur was anyone's guess. From what she'd read in the EMP book, solar storms were more predictable than something like a nuclear-EMP attack by North Korea, Iran, or one of the other countries that didn't like the United States very much.

Timing a bug-out, she determined, was critical to its success. In a perfect world, they'd have a destination, Colton would've been home, and the family would've left hours before the solar storm hit. If nothing happened, then they had a night or two away from home as a family getaway. They could always go back after the threat passed.

If you bugged out too late, which she now realized they had, you'd face masses of people with the same idea. The whole concept of sheltering-in-place might make sense in a bad storm, but in a catastrophic event like this once-in-a-lifetime solar storm, Madison realized that societal collapse occurred much faster than anyone could imagine. She'd seen the signs before, and after, the power grid went down.

The Wagoneer bounced through the field as Colton ran through ruts in the dirt and hopped over potholes in the ground. This jarred Alex, who let out a grumble, as most teenagers awoken from their slumber might do. Colton continued through the fields, looking for an entry point back onto the road.

"Maddie, I don't like the looks of this," said Colton as several people started toward them. "We're attracting too much attention." Having one of the few operating vehicles in town was another reason to bug out before everything collapsed, thought Madison.

"What if we turn around and find another way?" asked Madison, but as she glanced in the side-view mirror, she answered her own question. People were gathered behind them and walking behind the truck. Soon, they would be surrounded.

They began to hear shouts as suddenly people began running toward them from the parked cars on Vaughn Road. Two men had reached their tailgate and began to tug at the tarp that covered the extra gasoline and the generator.

"Colton, we've got to do something," urged Madison. Colton pressed the gas and swerved to the left, abandoning the attempt to regain access to the road, instead heading towards the open fields surrounding the baseball diamonds.

"I'm gonna try to make it to the asphalt driveway that circles around the pavilions over there," said Colton as the rear end of the Wagoneer swayed in the dust, kicking up dirt and gravel on their pursuers. The truck hit the asphalt road at an angle, causing it to catch and sway back and forth. But Colton gained the much-needed traction to speed up and put distance between them and the chasing mob of at least three dozen people.

Alex, fully awake again, shouted, "There, Daddy, to the left of those power poles. There's an opening by those big rocks."

Colton picked up speed and burst onto the field again, bouncing the truck up and down until he finally slowed his pace. Madison glanced back and saw that the pursuers had given up the chase.

"We're good, Colton," she said, bracing her hands against the dashboard. "You can slow down now."

Colton reacted slowly to her suggestion, his hands gripping the wheel to the point his knuckles were white.

Madison reached over and rubbed his shoulder. "Honey, we're good."

Colton let the air out of his lungs and shook his head, acknowledging that the threat was over. He found his way through the large rocks and onto Vaughn Road.

"Colt, do you wanna pull over somewhere and catch your breath? Maybe grab a bottle of water?" asked Madison. She could tell Colton was shaken by the incident.

"Nah, but thanks, guys," he replied. "Let's keep rollin'. Somehow, I think the farther we get away from the city, the better it'll be."

Madison leaned over and kissed her husband on the cheek. She rubbed his neck and shoulders for a while to help him release some tension and to remind him that she loved him. She studied the face of the man she'd loved for so many years.

They were more at risk than she realized. Their operating vehicle stocked full of food and supplies was one of the most prized possessions on earth right now. People would stop at nothing to take away these things. Madison was prepared to make the tough choices. She vowed that she would protect, and defend, the most prized possession in her mind—her family—whatever it took.

CHAPTER 4

DAY FIFTEEN
7:35 a.m., September 23
Loveless Motel and Café
Highway 100
Belle Meade, Tennessee

Colton carefully approached the intersection with Highway 100. The NHC Assisted Living Center to their right had been looted. He took a double take to confirm there were two dead bodies decomposing in their hospital gowns, lying facedown at a side entrance. He immediately began to speak, attempting to draw the girls' attention away from the morbid sight like a good dad would do when traveling on the interstate to avoid their laying eyes on a dead critter in the road.

"We'll take a left here at the church and it should be a quarter mile or so past the Loveless Café," said Colton. He looked both ways out of habit and turned to the west and the entrance to the Natchez Trace Parkway. They passed a family of four walking down the road, pushing shopping carts with all of their worldly belongings.

Colton slowed the truck as the Loveless Café came into view. For nearly seventy years, the Loveless Motel and Café had been a fixture in southwest Nashville, known for its refuge as a cozy home away from home and its Southern comfort food.

In the 1950s, Highway 100 was the primary route between Nashville and Memphis two hundred miles to the west. Lon and Annie Loveless began a small business serving the travelers meals through the front door of their home, usually at picnic tables adorned with red-and-white tablecloths in their front yard.

As their business grew, the couple elected to expand their private home into the Loveless Motel and Café. Lon ran the motel and was responsible for smoking the meats while Annie whipped up batches of her homemade preserves and made-from-scratch biscuits.

Over time, the Loveless Café became world famous and had been featured on *The Today Show*, *Martha Stewart*, and *The Ellen DeGeneres Show*. For seventy years, it remained true to its origins, serving travelers across the rural South who enjoyed the backroads leading to hidden treasures as opposed to the interstates, which zipped them from city to city.

It was the sight of the current visitors to the Loveless Café that forced Colton to bring the Wagoneer to an abrupt stop, throwing Alex forward in her seat, and she slammed into the back of Madison's.

"Daddy!" she immediately protested.

"Sorry, look," he said. Colton pulled off the shoulder under a canopy of oak trees and shut off the motor. Thus far, they hadn't been noticed.

The parking lot in front of the Loveless Café was filled with military vehicles and construction trucks. A dozen uniformed National Guardsmen were huddled under a tent, drinking coffee.

Beyond the motel, several soldiers were setting up pylons at the exit off the Natchez Trace Parkway. Farther down, a military Humvee was parked sideways across the road, blocking access. The entrance to the Natchez Trace was not blocked, but Colton would have to drive past the entire contingent to get there. He recalled the provisions of the martial law order signed by the President, which provided for the confiscation of operating vehicles and all weapons.

"Should we go for it?" asked Madison. "We're not bothering anyone. We could just explain that—"

"I don't trust this at all, Maddie," replied Colton, cutting her off in mid-sentence. "It's a different world now. Although this looks like an official military exercise, it could be designed to entrap people like us. It's not worth the risk."

Madison began to unfold the map as Colton continued to study the activity in the parking area. The majority of the soldiers appeared to be preoccupied, focused more on their coffee and playful banter than what was going on around them. The Wagoneer was not well hidden and could have easily been spotted if they were paying attention.

Colton leaned over to study the map with Madison as they sought an alternative entrance to the Natchez Trace when someone tapped on the rear passenger window. Alex shrieked and Colton immediately fumbled for his weapon. His clumsy hands tried to find the grip and knocked it onto the floorboard of the Wagoneer. As he frantically reached down, another knock came, this time at his window.

"Hey, mister," said a young boy's voice. "Y'all gonna get busted by them po-pos."

Colton looked up into the young boy's face with his nose just inches from the truck's window. He was maybe ten or eleven years old and wore a Tennessee Titans jersey bearing the number 29 of star running back DeMarco Murray. He didn't see a weapon, or anyone else, so he slowly opened the window with his left hand while he finally found his gun with his right.

"How's it goin'?" asked Colton harmlessly.

"All right, I guess," said the boy matter-of-factly. "You know, if they was payin' attention, they'd be on you like white on rice."

Colton turned his attention to the National Guard personnel, who were beginning to make their way out of the tent and were now gathering around their vehicles. He needed to make a decision. He returned his attention to the young boy.

"We need to get on the Natchez Trace and head south, but it looks like they're gonna block the road."

"Yup, they is," said the boy. "They come in last night and took over the Loveless. I went over there to get sumptin' to eat, and they run me off. I heard 'em say they was gonna close off the roads."

Colton's mind raced. If they were gonna drive past the military in full view, they needed to do so now before they loaded up into their vehicles. There wasn't another entrance to the Natchez Trace for many miles and it would require them to backtrack another fifteen miles or so.

The youngster interrupted his thoughts. "You can go through our yard if'n you want."

"What, what do you mean?" asked Colton.

"Well, my pa had a trail cut through dem woods which comes out on the Trace. He used it for his four-wheeler when he went fishin' over there at Haselton's pond. Your truck will fit."

Colton studied the activity at the Loveless one last time. It was worth a try.

"Are you sure your father won't mind?" asked Colton.

The boy became morose and lowered his head. There was a moment of awkward silence before he spoke again.

"He dead. They kilt him a week ago at the Loveless. He worked there as a cook and was watching over things for the owners when a bunch of white men come and kilt him. There wasn't nuthin' to steal, but they kilt him anyway."

Colton didn't know what to say as he became overcome with emotion. Alex began to sniffle, as did Madison. This young man had lost his father barely a week ago to a senseless murder. Yet, here he was willing to help a *white man* protect his family from possible arrest.

"What's your name, young man?" asked Colton.

"LaRon."

"Are you alone, LaRon?"

"Nah, I've got my ma. We're makin' out okay 'cause Pa brung da food over to our place. I dug holes and hid it on the property so as nobody could find it. Plus, I still walk over to the pond and fish."

"Colton," interrupted Madison as she regained her composure, "we've got to do something."

Colton looked up and saw the olive drab green fork trucks begin to unload barriers from the flatbeds. He reached over his shoulder and pulled the door lock up.

"Hop in, LaRon, and lead the way."

Colton started the Wagoneer, which couldn't be heard over the roar of the diesel motors at the Loveless Café. He slowly backed up about a hundred yards, where LaRon instructed him to turn into a gravel driveway leading into the trees across the road. They wound their way through the woods until they entered a clearing.

A white craftsman-style home with a black metal roof stood in front of a barn and a couple of small storage buildings. Several raised planter beds full of vegetables were off to the left next to a well with a hand-pump. Colton guessed the home had been built in the twenties or thirties.

As the Wagoneer approached the home, LaRon's mother emerged with two young girls behind her white skirt. She pointed a double-barreled shotgun at the truck. LaRon immediately jumped out of the truck and waved his arms.

"Whatcha doin', boy?" shouted LaRon's mother as she lowered the shotgun, much to Colton's delight. He had his weapon ready to return fire but dreaded the prospect of a gunfight with the widow.

"Ma, I'm just givin' dem directions to the Trace. Dey gonna cut through da woods."

"Then go on now," she shouted. "We don't want dem soldiers up here gittin' in our bidness. Go on!" She swung the barrel of the shotgun to the right side of the house, where Colton could see the entrance to the trail.

"Okay," shouted Colton through his window. "We're leavin' now. Thank you!"

LaRon stood there with his thumbs tucked in his jeans pockets. He managed a smile and waved to Colton.

Colton put the truck in drive and started to pull away. He glanced in the rearview mirror. Alex was in the backseat, frantically digging around in the rear of the Wagoneer. She apparently found what she was looking for.

"Daddy, stop, wait!" she shouted. Before Colton could come to a complete stop, she opened the rear door and bounded out and around the Jeep.

Alex walked toward LaRon, and his mother instinctively raised her shotgun in Alex's direction.

"Alex, what are you doin'?" asked Colton.

Alex approached Laron and asked, "Do you like comic books?"

"Sure do!"

"Do you like *The Walking Dead*?"

"I love zombie ones!"

Alex gave LaRon the comic book given to her by Jimmy Holder. It was the one-hundredth issue of *The Walking Dead* series.

Tears of joy began to roll down LaRon's face. Alex leaned down and gave the young boy a hug. He might now be the man of the house, but inside, he was still just a boy.

CHAPTER 5

DAY FIFTEEN
10:00 a.m., September 23
Natchez Trace Parkway
Leiper's Fork, Tennessee

The Natchez Trace Parkway was a two-lane road running from Nashville to Natchez, Mississippi, an historic town located on the Mississippi River. This four-hundred-forty-mile highway, which locals referred to as the Trace, was traveled for hundreds of years by Indians who followed the early footpaths created by the foraging of bison, deer, and other large game.

When the first European explorers came to the region, led by Hernando de Soto, the path was well worn and later became a wilderness road followed by pioneers and settlers heading west out of Tennessee and Kentucky. Eventually, at the behest of a group of ladies' garden clubs in the South, the Natchez Trace became a part of the National Park Service in the late thirties.

The Trace followed and maintained the spectacular scenery along its route, including the preservation of the swamps and forests, by limiting access to only a handful of access points along the entire parkway.

Over the years, tales of buried treasure, ghost stories, outlaws, and witches became as much a part of the Trace as the road itself. Stories of the demise of the *Kentucks*, entrepreneurs who traveled to and from Natchez to sell their goods, at the hands of outlaws and Indians were commonplace. Then the brutal battles between the *rebs* and the *yanks* during the Civil War were remembered as the Union Army was bent on bringing the South to heel.

The Rymans were feeling better after hitting the open road. This morning, no ghosts of the Trace's violent past invaded their thoughts, and the encounters of the morning were already a distant memory. Mile after mile, the road dipped and turned gracefully through rich fields, grassy meadows, and trees whose leaves were beginning to turn into their autumns shades.

And there was no traffic. Not a single car coming or going. The dreamlike quality of being completely alone in the world was only interrupted on one occasion when a lone farmer, sitting atop a Tennessee Walking Horse, was seen herding cattle off in the distance.

"This is more like it, don't you agree, guys?" asked Colton.

The wind blew through Madison's hair and she stuck her head out slightly to catch a deep breath of fresh air. She loved this. In fact, she wondered why they couldn't find a place here to find a spot, plant roots, and make a new life.

Alex must've been thinking the same thing. "Daddy, maybe we could find a farmer around here to take us in. You know, sleep in the barn or something until things settle down and we can go home?"

Colton, who was maintaining a steady fifty miles an hour, wheeled the Wagoneer through a set of curves. As they entered a wooded area, he replied, "It does look inviting, honey, but we don't know any of these folks. What if we take a chance and drive up someone's driveway and find out they're dangerous? We could lose everything, including each other."

The open fields were suddenly gone and Colton continued to wind his way through the woods. The two-lane highway seemed tight as the shoulder of the road gave way to a steep embankment on both sides with no guardrail.

"I know that, Daddy, but we have to trust someone," replied Alex.

Colton had unconsciously picked up speed during his conversation and was now going over sixty when he rounded a bend in the road.

"Whoa!" he exclaimed as he let off the gas and shoved on the brake pedal. He immediately checked his mirrors and looked for an option to pull off the road. There wasn't one.

The three cyclists toting heavy backpacks and bedrolls apparently were caught off guard as well. One rider overreacted and pulled over to the shoulder, losing his balance, which caused him and his now destroyed bicycle to tumble down the hill toward the overgrown brush. The other cyclists stopped to assist their friend, but hurled curse words and shook their fists at Colton.

"Sorry," yelled Madison as Colton continued to drive past them.

"Should we stop to help them?" asked Alex.

"I didn't run him off the road," replied Colton. "Again, it's like I was saying. We can't take the risk. They'll figure it out."

The family drove in silence for several minutes as the road opened up into farmland again. As they approached an intersection that included an exit to Leiper's Fork, Madison saw something that was straight out of the eighteen hundreds.

"Look, to the right," she exclaimed. "Slow down for a minute, Colt."

Colton slowed the truck at the overpass and the Rymans watched as four sets of horses and carriages came down Highway 46 toward Leiper's Fork.

"Hey, their wagons are loaded with baskets of vegetables," said Madison.

"Another one is holding piglets!"

Colton came to a full stop at the overpass and the Rymans exited the Wagoneer to take in the spectacle. Colton whispered into Madison's ear, "Help me keep an eye out for those bicyclers, okay."

Madison nodded and turned her attention back to the wagon train.

"Hey," shouted Alex to a teenage boy in overalls who led the first wagon with another, younger boy. "Where y'all goin'?"

As the wagon made its way through the underpass, the younger boy hollered, "Ya sure are purdy!"

Alex blushed and smiled at the boy, whose brother immediately gave him a playful shove. He then responded to Alex's question.

"There's a market in Leiper's Fork. We're takin' this stuff to sell or trade."

Alex leaned over the guardrail as the first wagon passed beneath them. The next buckboard contained the boys' parents.

"Y'all could get a pretty penny for that truck," said the father. "In fact, I'll trade you my whole last wagon full of pigs fer it. You can have the wagon too and the horses. I tell you what else, you can have them young'uns drivin' it also. But you gotta feed 'em!"

The man started roaring in laughter, but the woman on the seat next to him didn't seem to think it was as funny. She grabbed his green John Deere cap off his head and began to swat him with it.

"You lay off them young'uns," she hollered. "Or I'll whoop ya!" That last part echoed from underneath the bridge as the horses continued to clomp their way to Leiper's Fork.

"There you go, Alex," started Colton. "I could make a deal with Farmer Bob there, trade for the pigs and the wagon and the young'uns. Who knows? I could marry you off to the boy and get a dowry or somethin'."

"Daddy!"

"Colton Ryman! You stop that, or I'll whoop ya," shouted Madison as she chased Colton around the truck.

THANK YOU FOR READING THIS EXCERPT OF
TURNING POINT, book three of The Blackout series.

The entire six book series is available on Amazon.com.

You may purchase signed copies, paperback and hardcover editions of Bobby Akart's books on www.BobbyAkart.com.